Lydia Barnes
and the
Blood Diamond
Treasure

Heather Gemmen Wilson

wesleyan
publishing
house

Indianapolis, Indiana

Copyright © 2007 by Heather Gemmen Wilson
Published by Wesleyan Publishing House
Indianapolis, Indiana 46250
Printed in the United States of America

ISBN: 978-0-89827-350-2

Library of Congress Cataloging-in-Publication Data

Wilson, Heather Gemmen.
  Lydia Barnes and the blood diamond treasure / Heather Gemmen Wilson.
    p. cm.
  Summary: Lydia, a teen from Indianapolis, accompanies her father, a
consultant for Global Relief and Outreach, to Monrovia, Liberia, where she
and Ben, the son of medical missionaries, go on a danger-filled treasure
hunt that they hope will lead to diamonds.
  ISBN 978-0-89827-350-2
  [1. Missionaries--Fiction. 2. Treasure hunt (Game)--Fiction. 3. Fathers
and daughters--Fiction. 4. Christian life--Fiction. 5. Medical
care--Fiction. 6. Monrovia (Liberia)--Fiction. 7. Liberia--Fiction. 8.
Mystery and detective stories.] I. Title.
  PZ7.W6952Lyd 2007
  [Fic]--dc22
                                    2007014315

# Contents

| 1. | X Marks the Spot | 6 |
| 2. | Expect the Unexpected | 15 |
| 3. | Get a Clue | 25 |
| 4. | A Whole New World | 32 |
| 5. | Not Alone | 39 |
| 6. | The Temple of Justice | 51 |
| 7. | The Dad Factor | 58 |
| 8. | Hink Stink | 67 |
| 9. | Diamonds Are Forever | 74 |
| 10. | Absolutely Crazy | 85 |
| 11. | You'd Better Believe It | 94 |
| 12. | Dark Shadows | 103 |
| 13. | Off the Beaten Path | 112 |
| 14. | The Gift That Came Back | 123 |
| 15. | Cross-Eyed | 131 |
| 16. | Slimy Snot | 140 |
| 17. | Mother Lode | 148 |

For Larry,

who believes in the impossible

# A Note to You

When I was a girl living in the wide-open spaces of Oklahoma, I loved mystery stories. Sometimes, as I followed the adventures of my hero, Nancy Drew, the story was so intense that I could barely turn the pages to see what would happen next. Little did I know that I would someday experience many similar adventures of my own.

When I became a follower of Jesus, he opened the world to me. I began to see that it was not just storybook heroes who could have adventures—regular kids like I was could go out and do amazing things to make the world a better place. Remember, when you and I pray the Lord's Prayer saying "Thy will be done on earth as it is in heaven," God wants *us* to make that happen!

Now I'm pleased to introduce you to a wonderful new hero named Lydia Barnes. I know you'll be thrilled to follow her adventures in faraway places like Africa, Jamaica, and Jerusalem. As you do, remember this amazing truth—*Kids can change the world!*

I hope this book will be the beginning of your own adventure. I am looking forward to hearing about the awesome, creative things *you* will do to make a difference in your community and in the world.

Jo Anne Lyon
Executive Director
World Hope International

# 1
# X Marks the Spot

She never expected the breath of a lion to be sweet. Correction. She never expected the breath of *lions* to be sweet . . . or so close. Lydia Barnes backed away from the two giant cats staring at her, keeping her eyes glued to their twitching tails. She didn't dare to scream. She didn't dare to turn her head to search for an escape route. Step by step she inched back—and her terror was like a giant wave about to crash over her. Lydia couldn't help imagining those monstrous teeth sinking into the flesh of her throat.

The golden fur of the female rippled in the sunlight as she leapt, and the boom of the male's voice vibrated like a mighty motor. Lydia scrambled out of the path of deadly claws just in time. She ran. No more baby steps. She hiked up her skirt—why in the world was she wearing a skirt?—and nearly flew to the Land Rover she could see in the distance, where her mom was waiting.

She was too slow. The lions pounced in front of her, blocking her path. When Lydia whirled around, she saw a dozen more slinking out of the tall grass toward her.

"Mom!" Lydia screamed. "Mom!"

But when she turned around once again, the green Land Rover was gone. She could see only the dust rising in a cloud along the road.

"Nooo!"

The lions rushed toward her. . . .

Lydia opened her eyes. She was staring into the face of her dad. He looked worried.

"Did you have a nightmare, Peachoo?" he asked. He always called her that. Who knew why?

Lydia shrugged, still a bit confused.

"You were making more of a racket than Mrs. Hinkle," he said.

Lydia craned her neck to peek between the seats to catch a glimpse of the woman her dad had hired to be her tutor. Mrs. Hinkle—a skinny old lady who wore her hair up in a tight bun— was wearing a long, royal purple skirt and a lime-green blouse with ruffled sleeves that made her arms look like white sticks. She was snoring loudly, and her orange cat-eye glasses bounced up and down on her nose.

The first time Lydia met Mrs. Hinkle, the woman looked Lydia up and down, literally walking around her, making little grunting noises. "So this is she, eh?" Mrs. Hinkle said to Frank, using proper grammar, of course. "I can see I'm going to have to keep a close eye on this one." Then she pulled out a CD labeled "School Rocks!" in purple handwriting and gave it to Lydia. It turned out to be an awesome collection of classic and contemporary rock songs, Christian and mainstream, that all had something to do with learning.

Lydia wasn't sure what she thought of Mrs. Hinkle yet, but being tutored had to be better than going to regular school.

Now that she and her dad would be jetting around the world rather than living in the suburbs of Indianapolis, Lydia would never have to go to school again. Her father had accepted a job as senior consultant—whatever that meant—for Global Relief and Outreach (GRO), and he would be going from country to country to check on the work of missionaries and to offer support.

This was trip number one—Lydia's first airplane ride since the trip to Africa when she was six. She didn't think she was nervous, but then she hadn't had a nightmare in ages. *I'm just surprised I wasn't dreaming about diamonds,* she thought. Ben, the missionary kid who lived in Liberia with his parents, had e-mailed her about some treasure hunt he wanted them to do together when she got there. He had found some old map and was convinced the hidden treasure had to be diamonds.

Lydia had teased Ben at the time but was secretly glad for a reason to hang out with him. He sounded cool. And good looking. And if he turned out to be right about the diamonds, that would be all the better. *I could use a little bling-bling,* she thought.

"Are there diamonds in Liberia, Dad?" Lydia asked as she rested her head on his shoulder. She stared at the video screen on the seatback in front of her. The screen rotated through several channels that gave information about the flight in different languages. It told how high they were, how cold it was outside, when they left, and when they were expected to arrive—plus it showed a digital map marking their exact location. Somehow the information was comforting to Lydia. Even more comforting was the illustrated instructions she found in a pocket on the seatback in front of her that explained what to do in case of a crash. She felt completely prepared for anything.

"Yes, there are diamonds in Liberia," her dad said. "Unfortunately."

"Why is that bad?"

"Well, Liberia produces almost no diamonds, but billions of dollars worth of diamonds pass through it."

"Why is that bad?" Lydia asked again. Her dad knew everything. When she was little, he had traveled from country to country providing accounting and consulting services to Christian ministries—and still told wild stories about those days. Someone else's dad would have gotten on the airplane, taken a taxi to the hotel, stared at paperwork for a few days, and then come home.

Her dad would end up getting lost on a dirt bike in the African bush or wrestling a crocodile in South America to save some little kid.

"Mining can be done only by people who have a mining license," he said. "That reminds me, when your mom and I took you to Guinea all those years ago, Mom spotted a beautiful heart-shaped diamond in the marketplace, and she batted her eyelashes until I agreed to buy it. She wanted to make a necklace out of it for you, my sweet, as an heirloom."

"She did?" Tears suddenly shot into Lydia's eyes, but she quickly pulled her emotions back in check.

"Yes," her dad said, "but before I pulled out my wallet to buy it, I asked to see the mining license—which the guy didn't have."

"Huh?"

"He didn't have a license to sell diamonds. He was probably trying to sell me blood diamonds."

"Blood diamonds?"

The plane bumped a little, but her dad kept talking. He didn't seem to notice the turbulence. "Some African countries, like Sierra Leone, harvest diamonds like you harvest mulberries from the back yard," he replied, "—which is bad because of environmental issues, but even worse because of how it supports the rebels who have killed so many innocent people."

"Rebels?" Lydia asked, glad that the bumping seemed to be over for now.

"Rebels are soldiers who fight against the government."

"So you didn't buy it?" she asked.

"Buy what?"

Lydia couldn't believe he forgot what they had been talking about. "The diamond Mom wanted to get me!" she said.

"As much as I wanted to please my girls, I had a responsibility first to God. I just couldn't be part of the rebel cause, even in an indirect way," her dad said.

Whatever.

"So if I find diamonds in Liberia, I can't do anything with them?" Lydia asked.

"Diamonds are not exactly lying about, so I don't think this will be an issue for you."

"It might be." Lydia leaned closer to him. "Don't tell anyone, but Ben VanderHook found a map to a real diamond mine. He told me!"

"Well," her dad said, "it's true that Liberia is a prime location for such a hidden treasure."

Lydia smiled. The best thing about her dad, Frank Barnes—besides being so adventurous—was that he took kids seriously. Maybe because he was such a kid himself. Take yesterday for example: Lydia had introduced him to YouTube, and he had stayed up until two in the morning watching silly video clips like NumaNuma and *Star Wars* spoofs.

"Amazing stuff!" he'd said the next morning as he hurriedly packed, making them almost miss their plane. "I mean, there's real talent out there. You don't need to be Britney Spears to get attention anymore. Anyone with a webcam and a little flair can be famous. Amazing."

She knew he would take this treasure hunt seriously, too. "But why would someone make some weird map to it?"

"Good question," her dad said. "Why wouldn't they just harvest the treasure themselves?"

"Maybe they thought the mine would cave in, and they didn't want to risk it themselves."

"Or maybe they didn't have a miner's license," her dad said.

"Anyway," Lydia said, "we're going to try to hunt it down."

Lydia had an adventurous side, too. She thought of herself as a female clone of Frank Barnes, and she couldn't wait for escapades of her own. If only she could get her dad to realize that she had grown up so he wouldn't be so protective of her all the time.

"Where did Ben get the map?" her dad asked.

"He found it hidden under the floorboards in his room," Lydia said. "He noticed PRVB24 on the top right-hand corner in very small letters. He decided to look up Proverbs 2:4, and it turned out to be that passage that says something about seeking a hidden treasure."

"Yes, 'search for wisdom as for hidden treasure,'" Frank murmured.

That was the major difference between Lydia and her dad. He was the most passionate Christian she'd ever known. He had the whole Bible memorized, it seemed, and he was always talking about his faith with others. It got embarrassing at times. It wasn't that Lydia didn't have faith. She believed in God and all that. It was just that she didn't want to talk about Him all the time.

Besides, if she were perfectly honest, Lydia wasn't entirely sure God would always be there for her when she needed Him. He hadn't been there for her mom.

"Right," Lydia said. "Well, he figured it must be a treasure map, so he looked at every speck of the map until he found an X."

"He really found one?"

"Yep," Lydia said. "It was tiny and black, so he hardly noticed. But he finally found the X right in the middle of the map over a post office."

Her dad leaned toward her, obviously interested. "And then what?"

The flight attendant walked by pushing a cart and glanced at Lydia. "Oh, you're awake!" she said, smiling broadly. "I saved you a snack." The woman pulled a small box out of the cart and handed it to Lydia. "The cookies might even be warm still."

Lydia dove right into it. "Mmmm!" she said. "This is sooo good! Thank you!"

"Lydia!" her dad said as soon as the woman walked on. "What did Ben do?"

"Oh!" Lydia said with her mouth full. "He went to that post office and looked all over the grounds for some clue. But it was impossible. The building was basically gone—only the cement blocks were left. I guess during the war the bad guys shot everything, even lampposts—"

"Wait," her dad said. "How do you know all this? You haven't even met Ben yet."

"You're the one who gave me his e-mail address, remember? And after that we started IMing."

"What's that?" Frank asked.

"Dad! Instant messaging! Everyone does it."

"Oh. Okay. Go on."

"Anyway," Lydia paused dramatically, "Ben finally realized the post office wouldn't lead him to the next clue, so he went to a newly opened post office a few miles away to see if he could find any clues there."

"He's tenacious, isn't he?" her dad said.

"Whatever that means," Lydia said—and then quickly continued before her dad could start reciting the dictionary definition and Latin root of the word. "Anyway, he asked them what happened to the mail that had been in the destroyed post office."

"What did they say?"

"They said most of it had been lost, but they were sorting through what had been recovered."

"Recovered?" her dad asked.

"They basically took the mail strewn all over the floor of the old building and tried to read the labels. The bad guys—"

"The rebels," her dad corrected.

"The rebels weren't interested in letters," Lydia said. "They were looking for packages that had items of value."

"Ladies and gentlemen," said a voice over the loudspeaker, "this is your pilot speaking. We expect a bit of turbulence in a few moments. The seatbelt sign has been turned on. We ask that you all return to your seats and fasten your seatbelts."

Lydia quickly buckled up and stared at her dad.

"Don't worry, honey," he said. "It happens all the time. What did Ben do next?"

Lydia looked out the window and watched the airplane lights flashing in the dark sky. "He didn't even know what he was look-ing for, so he offered to help them sort. They were surprised, but they let him."

"Did he find anything?"

Lydia turned back to her dad. "Mostly junk that wasn't even readable, but he did find some mail that had existing addresses. He was so excited about that." Lydia smiled, remembering the IM where Ben had gushed: "im so happy i cud kiss u . . . wat a rush to give sum1 news about sum1 they lost for so long!"

"I mean about the treasure hunt," her dad urged.

"Oh. Yes. He found a bunch of mail addressed to Wisdom, PO Box 24. The ladies there loved him by then, so they let him take it all."

"What kind of mail?"

"Some old catalogs with church pews and stuff like that, some requests to donate money to different Christian ministries, a postcard, some church newsletters."

"And that's all?"

Lydia sighed. "Be patient," she said. "One envelope in the pile caught his eye."

"Why? What was so special about it?"

"It was just a normal envelope, but it was from the Proverbs 24 Group."

"Ooh!" Frank said. "Proverbs 2:4—just like what he found on the map!"

"That's right," Lydia said, glad that he was listening. "Ben opened up the envelope right away, of course."

Her dad was all but in her seat. "What was it?"

At that moment two things happened. First, Lydia turned quickly to see Mrs. Hinkle move back in her chair and pretend to be asleep. Second, the plane dropped suddenly and everyone screamed.

# 2
# Expect the Unexpected

E ven the Top Thrill Dragster roller coaster at Cedar Point wasn't this scary. Lydia held on to the armrests of her seat, turning her knuckles white, as the plane lurched up and down like a moth under a floodlight.

The plane dropped again, and the man sitting in front of Lydia nearly hit his head on the ceiling of the plane. He must not have buckled up. The flight attendants rushed from the back with their carts and locked them into position before strapping themselves into their jump seats.

"Daddy?" Lydia whispered without taking her eyes off the seatbelt sign above her.

She flinched when she felt his hand on her head, and momentarily wondered how he had been able to let go of . . . of what? There was nothing safe to hold on to.

This is how her mom must have felt.

Another big lurch, and the oxygen masks fell from the overhead compartment. Lydia screamed again.

"Lydia." Her dad's voice cut through her terror. "Put it on."

She turned her head and saw him smiling at her as he demonstrated how to position the oxygen mask on her face. He looked like the people on the illustrations in the seat pocket who smiled their way through a plane crash. His calmness helped to settle her nerves so she could follow the instructions.

"Daddy, are we going to die?" Lydia asked. Her voice sounded hollow through the mask.

"We're going to be okay," he said—and the plane lurched again. "No matter what happens."

Lydia heard a woman scream. "How do you know?" she asked.

He winked at her.

"Dad!"

"God's got everything under control, honey." More people were screaming and the plane still seemed out of control, but her dad didn't look scared at all. Lydia wondered how he, of all people, could be calm. His own wife had died in a plane crash. "He'll protect us from harm if He wants to."

"If He wants to?" Lydia asked.

Frank touched Lydia's forehead. "Pray, Lydia. Trust Him."

Lydia slammed her eyes closed and leaned back into her seat as she silently shouted out to God for help. She thought of her mom, who must have been praying these same words before she died. *Are You even there, God? Do You really have everything under control?*

And then the turbulence stopped. Just as suddenly as it had started. The plane transformed from an unpredictable moth to a gliding hawk. Lydia felt like she was being pressed down into her seat as the plane leveled out.

She opened her eyes. "We're alive!"

Her dad laughed.

"Mrs. Hinkle, we're alive—" Lydia turned around to see the old lady clutching her knees up to her chest with her hands. Her bun had come loose and hair covered part of her face, but Lydia could still see terror all over it. At least Lydia wasn't the only chicken around. "Are you okay, Mrs. Hinkle?" Lydia asked.

The woman quickly smoothed her hair with her hands. "Not quite as exciting as bungee jumping, but still quite good."

An hour later Lydia ran up the jetway into the Brussels airport, thankful to see solid land. She even thought about getting down on the floor to kiss it. "I'm never flying again, Dad!" she said. "Never!"

"Well, at least not for six hours," her dad said. "We have a long layover."

After stepping out of the long jetway, almost everyone turned left. They were getting in line to talk to some government people in neat little glass booths. Nobody pushed or shoved like they did in the lunch line at Lydia's school. They stood patiently behind a white line on the shiny tiled floor until the government officers motioned them forward.

Lydia wanted to join them. Boring, maybe. But everyone turning left was staying in Belgium. Everyone turning right was heading to the transit area to wait for another plane.

Lydia and company turned right. Ugh.

"Six hours in this horrible place," Mrs. Hinkle said.

The hallway before them was long and empty. A moving sidewalk stretched through the hallway, but it wasn't moving. The floor was carpeted in this part of the airport, but it was gray and boring. The only interesting thing Lydia could see was a little green sign above a door that pictured a stick person running into a wall. Lydia figured it was supposed to be an exit sign.

"It's not so bad here, Gretchen," Frank said to Mrs. Hinkle. "The transit area right up those escalators is a gorgeous shopping center." Then he stopped and looked around at the concrete walls as if they were the Swiss Alps. "Did you know this airport was built by the German occupying forces during World War II?" He was giving a history lecture, and they hadn't even had time to go to the bathroom!

Lydia rolled her eyes.

"The Germans asked the citizens where the best place to build an airport would be, and they all pointed to the place where the fog was the worst." Frank laughed, clearly delighted at his own joke. Lydia sighed.

"This is educational, Lydia," Mrs. Hinkle scolded. "Pay attention."

"I don't really have to get back on that plane, do I?" Lydia asked her dad.

"Not that one," he responded. "We'll be on a different one."

"Can't we take a train or something?"

"Ooh! Ooh! Ooh!" Mrs. Hinkle twittered. "It looks like our girl needs some geography lessons."

Lydia groaned and dug into her backpack until her hand landed on the cold white object she craved—her iPod. Mrs. Hinkle proceeded to explain that taking a train would be possible, though time-consuming, until they reached the Strait of Gibraltar. They'd have to take a boat from France or Italy across the Mediterranean Sea. "And that would only get you into Africa—"

Lydia stuck the buds into her ears and declared that she was going to the bathroom. She didn't need to turn around to know that Mrs. Hinkle was glaring at her through those orange cat-eye rims and that her dad was still gawking around like a tourist at the Indy 500 racetrack. Within seconds her favorite band, Pillar, blasted peace into Lydia's frantic soul.

Once inside the restroom, Lydia took her time. She pulled the twin braids out of her thick, dark hair and rewove one long braid down the back. She washed her face and put on a dab of lip gloss—the only makeup her dad would let her wear. She stood in front of the mirror sideways and sucked in her belly—which stuck out just enough to drive her nuts—and pushed out her chest—which hardly made a difference. Still, she looked cute in her low-rider jeans and black T-shirt sporting a bright blue butterfly. She hoped Ben would approve.

When Lydia walked out of the bathroom ten minutes later, she didn't see her dad or Mrs. Hinkle anywhere. "Dad should get me a cell phone," she said out loud.

"Lydia should count her blessings for the good things she already has," her dad's voice said from behind her.

"Oh." Lydia turned around to find both adults resting on a bench, looking completely bored. "Sorry I took so long."

"No worries," her dad said. "All we've got is time."

"What are we going to do for six hours?" Lydia asked. "Can we go shopping?"

"I'd like to find a padded bench to sleep on," Mrs. Hinkle said. The scary thing was that she was serious. Lydia got a vision of the old lady spread out on a bench with one arm over her head, her nose in her armpit, and her thumb in her mouth. Yikes!

"I wouldn't mind doing a bit of exploring," her dad announced. He looked at his watch. "We may even have time enough to step foot outside the airport."

"Count me out," Mrs. Hinkle declared. "I'll catch you at the gate." She stood up and then quickly corrected herself. "That is, if you don't need me, Frank."

"That depends on Lydia, I guess," her dad replied. "Do you want to go into Brussels with me?"

"Sure." She certainly didn't want to stay with her teacher.

"That's my girl."

"You'd better not miss your flight," Mrs. Hinkle warned.

"Let's go, Lyd," Frank said with a jump in his voice. "It's a twenty-minute bus ride to the city center."

"Don't lose your tickets!" Mrs. Hinkle hollered as they darted off. "Or your passports!"

"She's just what we need," Frank said with a laugh as they jogged toward the exit. "She'll keep us both in line."

"I wish you got a fun teacher," Lydia complained as she pulled her coat from her backpack.

"I tried!" her dad responded. "Hink must've used some of Mary Poppins' magic to get this job."

Lydia laughed. "'Hink'? I like it. It fits her. But what do you mean about Mary Poppins?"

"Mrs. Hinkle basically told me the job was hers," Frank said. "She said her dream has always been to get to Liberia, for some reason—and not just Liberia, but Monrovia, the capital, which is where we're going. And she's a highly skilled teacher. I didn't have the heart—or maybe the nerve—to refuse her. It doesn't matter, though. She's perfect."

What was perfect was the next four hours of Lydia's life. She and her dad boarded a city bus that wound its way to the center of the city. Despite a rain shower, Lydia could see small neat houses with tiled roofs and decorative iron fences. She saw some hotels and stores with names she recognized and others she had never heard of. Once they neared downtown, the buildings got taller and more majestic.

Lydia and her dad hopped out of the bus when it got to the end of the line and pulled out their umbrellas. They walked up and down the streets of Brussels, staring at the cathedrals and shops and redbrick roads as the cold rain fell steadily down.

If they had planned better, they might have gone to church. It didn't feel like a Sunday morning to Lydia, but many of the churches were holding services as she and her dad strolled through town. Frank was convinced that a service in one of the grand cathedrals would have been startlingly beautiful. Lydia privately enjoyed the fact that they were missing church for once.

Lydia's favorite site was the Grand Place, a gorgeous cobblestone plaza, surrounded by regal buildings, where crowds of people milled around admiring the life-size manger scene featuring real animals. Holiday music danced in their ears.

Lydia had no gloves and her hands were freezing, but the scene before her couldn't have been more magical. She felt as if she were entering a storybook tale that ended with the words "happily ever after." Adding to the exotic feel of the experience was the sound of people speaking all around her in French and Dutch. Lydia's dad kept trying to start up a conversation with her, but Lydia shut him down. She didn't want anyone to hear her American accent and realize she didn't belong here. She wished she had a pair of cute knee-length boots and a big knit scarf to better fit in with the trendy European crowd.

Finally, and with little time to spare, Lydia and her dad headed back to the airport. "The security line had better not be long," he said.

It was. They had cruised through the passport checkpoint thinking all was well, but the line for the security check went clear to the other side of the concourse. The line moved quickly, however, and they moved past a deluxe chocolate stand toward a giant television screen showing an animated film about how to place items on the security conveyor belt—which would take their stuff through an X-ray just like a conveyor belt at the grocery store would take their stuff  toward the cashier. Lydia thought the characters on the film looked like people from *Monsters, Inc.*

Lydia and her dad were almost up to the conveyor belt when they heard a man with a proper British accent speaking in a loud voice. "I'm a development worker, for goodness' sake," he told the security guards, who were cuffing him. They quickly led the tall, sandy-haired man toward a doorway marked *Police/Politie*.

"Hmm," Frank said. "They're taking him into the security area."

Lydia looked quickly at her dad. "Dad! We're development workers! Will they—"

"Shh . . ." he said, listening closely.

"Sure you're a development worker," a burly officer was saying to the British man. "Somebody in Guinea thinks otherwise."

The man in line behind Frank leaned in toward them and whispered in Frank's ear, and Lydia suddenly lost all interest in the spectacle in front of her.

"Are you Christian missionaries?" the man asked with a British accent.

To Lydia's shock and horror, her father nodded and shook the stranger's hand. "Frank Barnes," he said. "Global Relief and Outreach."

"Good organization," the man said. "I know Cynthia Bell very well."

Cynthia Bell was the executive director of GRO—Frank's boss. Lydia had heard lots of fun stories about the woman and couldn't wait to meet her in Monrovia. She was coming to visit the VanderHooks the same time Lydia and her dad would be there.

The men remained silent for a moment as they watched the man ahead of them led away.

"That's my colleague," the stranger said. "We're from Physicians Outreach Ministries, and we suspected that we would be stopped here."

"Why? What's going on?" Frank asked.

"Too long a story. Where are you going?"

"Liberia," Frank answered. "The capital city, actually. Monrovia."

"I'd like you to take my backpack if I don't make it through," the man said.

Frank turned to look at him full in the face. So did Lydia.

"I suggest that you turn around so the guards won't associate us," the man said.

Lydia and her dad turned away slowly, but not before they saw his gentle eyes and soft smile. He didn't even look scared.

"If I don't make it through," the man continued, "take my backpack off the conveyor belt, if you can get away with it. It is full of antibiotics, antimalaria pills, and other medications. All perfectly legal. It's desperately needed in Guinea, but I don't want it to go to waste if I'm detained here. The people in Liberia could use it, too. Please take it with you."

"I can't do that," Frank said quietly, still not looking at the stranger.

Lydia was watching the man, though, and saw him nod a little. "I suppose I don't blame you," he said. *Duh!* Lydia knew that her dad was adventurous, but he wasn't stupid.

They were quiet for a moment.

"Would you like to search my bag?" the man asked after a moment. "We can step out of line. You'll see it contains nothing illegal."

Frank chuckled. "If you were hiding anything, I'm sure it would be well concealed. I'd better just leave it. I'm sure you'll make it through anyway."

"Not likely," the man said with a shrug. "We stumbled across some illegal diamond trading last time we were in Guinea, and even the authorities are in on it. They don't want us back."

"I'm sorry," said Frank.

Silence again.

Frank looked at his watch. The line inched forward.

Lydia started placing her few belongings on the conveyor belt.

"So, what kind of medicine did you say you've got in there?" Frank asked quietly.

Lydia groaned. He was going to do it. He was smart enough to know better but crazy enough to do it anyway. He probably even believed this guy's story. That was her dad's problem: too much faith! He always thought things would turn out all right and figured everyone in the world was trustworthy. Lydia could see her dad practically drooling when the man repeated the names of the medications—apparently Ben's dad needed these same drugs for his clinic.

The three of them had placed their items on the conveyor belt and were just about to walk through the security checkpoint.

"God be with you," the man said.

"And also with you," Frank replied.

Lydia stepped through the metal detector and handed her passport and ticket to the guard. He handed them back, and then her dad walked through. The guard glanced at Frank's passport, then waved him past. Behind them their new friend handed his passport to the security officer and immediately got pulled to the side. "We got the other one, boss," the officer called out to the guard who had arrested the first Brit.

"Well, get his stuff and bring him over," the boss replied.

Lydia picked up her backpack and looked at her dad. Frank picked up his own carry-on bag, and then, with one smooth motion, slung the British man's backpack over his shoulder and started walking.

# 3
# Get a Clue

**D**on't look back," Frank said.

Lydia didn't need to be told twice. She stared straight ahead and kept walking.

They walked briskly down the concourse for about fifty yards. "Okay," Frank said. "It doesn't look like anyone is after us. Come on, we have to run or we'll miss our plane."

They almost did miss it. The announcement for final boarding call was being made as they sped, out of breath, up to the Brussels Airlines agent at the boarding gate. She smiled at Frank and Lydia as she checked their boarding passes. "You just made it," she said with a French accent, and the two of them ran down the jetway. Everyone else was already on board.

Surprisingly, this plane was larger than the one that had carried them across the Atlantic Ocean. Lydia had figured it would be smaller, thinking not many people would want to go to Liberia. There were all sorts of people onboard—there were Blacks, and Whites, and some people that looked like they must have been from the Middle East. Some were dressed in African clothes and some in Western clothes; all were talking in various languages. Even though she seemed to be the only kid on board, Lydia didn't feel out of place at all. What she did feel uncomfortable about was sitting inside this huge metal thing that was somehow supposed to float in the sky.

A flight attendant directed Lydia to her seat: 26A—coach class, where they had no room to stretch. She looked behind her seat and saw Hink writing furiously in a notebook.

"Hi, Mrs. Hinkle," Lydia said.

"Oh!" Hink quickly slammed the book shut and stuffed it into her bag. "It's about time you showed up. I thought I'd be going to Africa without you."

"I'm afraid you're stuck with us," Frank said. He smiled at Hink and then sat down beside Lydia.

"What's going to happen to those men?" Lydia asked after they were buckled in.

"Man alive," her dad said, using the geeky, out-of-touch phrase he always did. Lydia had often tried to get him to say something cooler, but he never would. "I hope everything works out for them," he said.

"Me, too," Lydia said. "But let's see what's in the backpack." She hardly even noticed when the plane started moving.

Frank immediately unzipped it. "Whooo-eee!" he said. "This is incredible! We're in desperate need of this at the clinic."

"That's awesome, Dad," Lydia said. "Good job."

"Good job? It's better than that. Your dad can do anything!" he teased. "Say it: My dad rocks!"

The plane starting moving fast down the runway, but even so Lydia couldn't help giggling. She said, "My dad's crazy!"

The plane lifted off and began to climb.

"Enough about me," Frank said with a grin. "Tell me what was in Ben's envelope."

"Oh, yeah," Lydia said. She was glad he remembered. "We never finished that conversation."

"I'm waiting . . ."

Lydia laughed. "Inside the envelope was—" she paused dramatically, smiling meanly at her dad.

"Lydia, I'll ground you if you keep me waiting any longer," he threatened playfully.

"I'm up in an airplane. How can you ground me?"

Frank reached around and began tickling his daughter. "Tell me!" he growled.

"Okay, okay!" she squealed. "It was a weird little poem. A clue."

He stopped tickling. "Do you remember it?"

"Yes. Do you promise not to tell anyone?"

"Cross my heart."

Lydia grabbed a piece of paper and jotted the clue down and showed it to her dad.

JTEAM—let us ice bed on toll en.

"Ben doesn't get it, and neither do I," Lydia said.

"Interesting."

"Do you know what it means?" Lydia asked.

"Maybe it has something to do with Monrovian sports?"

"I don't know." Lydia shrugged. "I think the letters are scrambled, but I've spent so much time trying to unscramble them that now I'm worried it's another language."

"Yeah, that would be bad," her dad said. "We'll only be there for three weeks. That might not be enough time to learn Kpelle."

"Learn what?"

"One of the languages spoken in Liberia."

She might have had time to learn it on this flight, though. It lasted about ten thousand years, and Lydia just couldn't fall asleep. Even watching movies became boring after awhile.

When the announcement came that they were going to land in Faranah, Guinea—the stopover before Monrovia—Lydia didn't even care that they'd have to go through another takeoff and landing. "Just let me out of here!" she said under her breath.

"Flight attendants," the pilot said, as if hearing her, "please prepare for landing."

The huge airplane lurched down a bumpy runway and came to a stop. Lydia stood up and prepared to get off the plane. She bounced on her toes as she waited impatiently for each person in the twenty-five rows ahead of her to pull carry-on luggage out of the overhead bins. After what seemed like an hour, the line began to inch forward. She finally stepped into the doorway of the plane to feel a blast of hot African air in her face. It wasn't just the heat that surprised her; it was the smell and the taste and the feel. It was like stepping into a huge outdoor kitchen where someone was frying mushrooms in ginger oil—while tossing sand into the air. When she licked her lips, Lydia could feel grit. Everything was different from Indianapolis, or even Brussels. Her senses were suddenly wide awake, made alive by new sensations—and Lydia couldn't move.

"Go," her dad said from behind her and gave Lydia a nudge.

Lydia quickly descended the steps, breathing in the hot, humid air.

She followed the crowd into a dark and dirty room where guards were waiting to stamp their passports. If the Brussels checkpoint had seemed different from her school's lunch line because of its orderliness, this checkpoint was like the school cafeteria on steroids. Everyone seemed to be shoving and pushing and yelling and arguing. She wouldn't have been surprised to see a piece of pizza fly into someone's face—only it would probably have been some weird foreign food instead. The walls were once painted white, but now they were a dingy gray. The floor was rough, unpainted cement. The doorway to which the passengers were directed was shorter than her dad, made of wood, and painted an ugly brown.

They finally made it through security and moved into a waiting area that looked a little better than the last room, but still out-of-date. The seats were thinly padded metal benches, and the walls were a dingy yellow. The two grimy windows revealed a rough gravel parking lot outside the terminal.

"You'll never believe this—" her dad began, but then he interrupted himself. "Hey! Physicians Outreach Ministries!" He grabbed Lydia's hand and headed straight toward a fat, bald man who was about two inches shorter than Lydia. He was holding the hand of a skinny woman with big, poofy hair. They wore matching bright green T-shirts that said Physicians Outreach Ministries in big white letters. The fair-skinned pair was very noticable in the middle of this crowd of mostly black people.

Frank introduced himself and his companions, and the couple welcomed all three warmly. "Are you here to pick up two British development workers?" Frank asked.

"Yes! We are!" the man responded, clearly British himself. "It appears their plane just arrived."

"Were you traveling with them?" the woman asked.

Frank frowned. "I'm sorry to tell you this, but your friends were not on that plane. And they won't be on the next one, either." He explained what had happened at the Brussels airport.

The woman sank down and put her hand over her stomach.

Frank sighed deeply, so Lydia knew this would be difficult for him. He slung the treasured backpack off his shoulder. "Here is the bag they were carrying," he said, holding it out to the man. "Looks like you need it." Frank managed a smile.

The woman stared at him for a moment, and then jumped up and kissed him on the cheek, leaving a large red smear of lipstick.

Lydia laughed out loud. She wanted to say, "You're wearing more makeup than I am, Dad," but she knew better and stopped herself. This was an important moment, she could tell.

"Thank you! Oh, thank you!" the woman cried. "God bless you!"

The bald man beamed too and shook Frank's hand up and down, not letting go. He patted Lydia on the head several times as tears sprang from his eyes.

The Bonsons, as it turned out the couple was named, offered to stay at the airport until Frank and Lydia and Hink could reboard the plane several hours later. "We don't want to leave you alone in case the flight is cancelled," they explained. "You might be caught here for several days." Lydia glanced around and noticed that there were no pay phones or waiting taxicabs.

Dad happily accepted their offer and sat down for a long boring conversation on West African politics. Lydia tuned in again when they started talking about Liberia—or Monrovia, or whatever it was called—because that's where they were going.

"The motto on the Temple of Justice in Monrovia says 'Let Justice Be Done to All Men,'" Mr. Bonson was saying. "It's almost a joke because the only reason there is any order now is because the United Nations sent in soldiers."

"What's the Temple of Justice? Is that a church?" Lydia asked.

"No, it's a government building, kind of like a courthouse," Mr. Bonson explained.

"Why are there soldiers there?"

Mr. Bonson didn't seem annoyed by her questions at all. He answered them cheerfully. "The soldiers are all over, not just at the Temple of Justice. The UN had to send soldiers to Monrovia to straighten things out. It's a mess."

"The United Nations, or the UN," her dad explained, 'is a world-wide organization of governments that works for world peace."

"They sure have their work cut out for them in Liberia," Mr. Bonson said. "Charles Taylor must have sneered every time he saw those words, 'Let justice be done...'"

"It's like what you and Ben were talking about," Lydia's dad told her. "The last president, Charles Taylor, was corrupt, which means he misused his power. Soon there was no order at all."

"And Guinea was affected by his corruption, too," Mr. Bonson added. "The war spilled over from Liberia to Sierra Leone. The Sierrra Leonians took refuge in Guinea, and the rebels attacked them here. Terrible!"

Lydia tried to imagine the geography. All these little countries must be neighbors.

And so the conversation continued. Even the grumpy Mrs. Hinkle seemed to have a sudden interest in being social.

Lydia stood up to stroll around the tiny airport, trying to stay awake. They had been traveling for nearly twenty-four hours with only a few hours of sleep. She stayed in clear view of her overprotective dad—the same man who had just dodged airport security for a bag of medicine. "Stay close," he kept saying.

Lydia rolled her eyes and strolled around the rundown waiting room. She kept herself busy by silently repeating Mr. Bonson's words, trying to mimic his British accent.

Suddenly it struck her: The clue she had been staring at for hours and hours was not about sports. It was about something much more important than that. She glanced down at the letters she had scribbled for her dad—JTEAM—let us ice bed on toll en—and knew exactly what it said. Exactly.

# 4
# A Whole New World

The moment Lydia was back on board the airplane, fatigue won over excitement and she fell asleep.

Less than an hour later they landed in Liberia, and her dad had to shake her awake. "Wake up, Peachoo," he said. "It's time to meet the VanderHooks."

Lydia groaned and wiped the drool off her cheek. So much for looking cute when she met Ben. Still, she couldn't wait to meet him. He'd have to be impressed with her detective skills, if nothing else.

When she walked off the plane this time, she wasn't so surprised by the pungent African air and took more time to look around. She couldn't see much in the dark, but it was exciting to catch a glimpse of palm trees waving from the side of the tarmac. The only lights she could see were coming from the airplane and the small building they were walking toward, which must have been the airport.

Lydia stood with her father to have their passports checked — only to have others cut in front of them and press into them, just as they had in Guinea.

"Observe the process! Observe the process!" she heard guards shouting with thick Liberian accents as people pushed their way through the mob.

Like the airport in Guinea, the concrete walls and floors seemed to generate heat, the lights were dim, and the wooden stalls for the people who stamped their passports looked like something she could have built. Lydia was disgusted. This place wasn't even as nice as the grimy truck stop where she and her dad had eaten while driving to her grandmother's house last Christmas.

The passport agent asked them all kinds of questions, which Lydia could barely understand because of his accent. Finally Frank said, "We're with Global Relief and Outreach," and the agent waved them on.

Everyone was pushing their way through the little wooden doorway as a guard attempted to stop the flow and look at passports. Lydia clung to her father's arm, but Hink darted in front of them and flung her wiry little body through the door, looking as proud as a golden retriever after catching a frisbee.

On the other side of the door, people crowded together around a dirty old conveyor belt waiting for luggage.

Lydia spotted their bags first and began to reach for one when a short black man with a toothless smile came out of nowhere and started lifting it for her. "Wait, wait," he said. "I help you. You are my friend." He was wearing a suit and shiny black shoes. Lydia wondered how he managed to stay so clean in all this grime. She was about to hand over her suitcase when her dad stepped between her and the new "friend."

"We'll take care of it, thank you," Frank said kindly but firmly. He pushed the suitcase toward Hink and grabbed the other two— repeatedly refusing assistance from the men who hovered around them hoping to earn a buck.

With all three suitcases and all three carry-on bags safely in tow, Lydia, Frank, and Hink walked toward the door in the back of the room where customs agents waited to check the luggage.

"I need money," the female guard said as soon as they set the suitcases on the tables for examination. It seemed like she wanted them to pay her to approve their bags. That didn't seem right.

"No. No money," Frank said firmly.

"Go," the woman hissed angrily without even looking at the bags. "Just go."

They walked out the door into that heady African air and looked around for the three VanderHooks. Lydia, of course, was interested only in one of them. Within moments a tall white man and a short white woman strode calmly toward them—clearly not fitting in the chaotic surroundings—and smiling at Dad.

Lydia caught a glimpse of a boy walking behind them. Ben. She smiled nervously and thought of her hair. The braid had come halfway out, and Lydia was sure that she must have had lines on her face from leaning so heavily on her dad's shoulder on the plane. Her clothing was hopelessly rumpled. She felt like hiding behind her dad.

But then the boy stepped forward and Lydia saw him fully.

Why, oh why, hadn't she asked her dad for a picture of this guy? She had been expecting him to look like Brad Pitt or at least Jesse McCartney. Instead he looked about as cool as Ronald Weasley. He was shorter than she was, had longish black hair and a loopy grin. Lydia thought he might be Chinese. He wore ratty tennis shoes with a ratty T-shirt to match.

"Hey, Lydia!" the boy yipped in a high voice—and then moved up right smack beside her. "I'm Ben. I'm glad you're finally here."

She nodded and tried to smile, then moved closer to her dad, who nudged her in the ribs.

"Hello, Lydia," Mrs. VanderHook said. She was slim and sugary sweet. She, and her husband too, were as white as the first page of Lydia's composition notebook—which she had meant to write in during this trip—which meant Ben must have been adopted. "We're thrilled you're here," Mrs. VanderHook continued. "You're going to be such a blessing to us, I'm sure." The missionary turned to Hink. "And we're delighted to have a teacher among us as well."

Hink, who had been retying her bun, shook Mrs. VanderHook's hand. "Delighted," she said. If Lydia hadn't just spent twenty-some hours traveling with Hink, she would have thought her teacher was as "delighted" as a cat that had fallen in a toilet. But Lydia remembered Hink's constant chatter about Monrovia, and knew better. Mrs. Hinkle was thrilled to be here.

The question was, *why*?

Dad already knew the VanderHooks and quickly started up a conversation with Dr. VanderHook about the state of local travel.

"It's much better now that Charles Taylor is gone," the doctor was saying. Lydia was proud that she remembered who Charles Taylor was—the corrupt president. "United Nations peacekeepers declare the roads from here to Monrovia to be as calm as clouds in the sky. There are no more weapons on the streets, according to the UN. Even so, we have to keep alert."

"For what?" Lydia asked. Keeping alert at this point seemed impossible. Her eyes felt like they would fall out of her head if she didn't close her lids.

"This country is very poor," Dr. VanderHook said. "People are desperate. They know that Americans have more than they do—probably things that could save their lives. They'd do just about anything to get their hands on the food, medicine, and clothing that we have."

"Why don't we just give it to them?" asked Lydia.

Mrs. VanderHook laughed and put her arm around Lydia's shoulders. "I knew you'd be a blessing to us," she said kindly. "You're a girl after my own heart."

Lydia liked Mrs. VanderHook just fine, but she still felt silly being hugged. And she hated it when people tried to act like a mother to her. "I was just asking," Lydia said.

"And you were right, Lydia," her dad responded quickly. "We *are* here to help. But simply giving handouts doesn't build up the country. We are here to provide resources—"

Lydia rubbed her eyes and looked for a place to sit down. "I'm tired."

"Right," Dr. VanderHook said. "Wait here. I'll get the car."

It was midnight on Sunday here—which meant it was seven o'clock in the evening at home. But Lydia had hardly slept the whole time they were traveling. She nearly fell asleep as she stood there leaning against a post with her head resting on her backpack, not listening to the conversation around her.

Once she caught Ben staring at her, but she didn't care if she looked as goofy as Hink probably had during the layover in Brussels. At this point Lydia had lost all interest in trying to impress him. She did consider telling him about the riddle she solved, but didn't have the energy right now. She was tired and hot and annoyed by the smell of urine, which seemed to be everywhere. People outside the airport kept coming up to her, asking if she wanted to buy some ugly wooden figurines or tie-dyed shirts. All Lydia wanted was a shower and a bed.

Dr. VanderHook pulled his gray Nissan Pathfinder up to where the group was standing. It wasn't really a driveway or even a parking lot, just an open, gravelly space. The luggage easily fit into the trunk, even though Lydia's suitcase was almost as big as she was and weighed about twice as much. Lydia herself didn't fit so easily. She was squished between the two women in the backseat, and Ben was squished between the two men in the front seat. No one smelled very good, but the car was air-conditioned. Good thing. It was December, but December in the eastern hemisphere was like July in Indiana, only way more humid, even at night. Ugh.

Finally, the SUV pulled away from the airport and headed down one of the few paved roads. Dr. VanderHook kept tooting the horn to warn people walking along the road that he was coming. But even with that noise, Lydia quickly fell asleep.

An hour later they pulled up to the VanderHooks' home. It was a two-story concrete house, just off the main road. The homes that surrounded it were much smaller, and some resembled the run-down post office Ben had described. Everywhere Lydia looked, she saw people. No one mentioned how odd it was to see so many people outside this late at night, or what a bad neighborhood they were in, so Lydia kept her mouth shut.

Suddenly a man stepped out from the shadows of the VanderHooks' porch and started toward them. Lydia almost screamed, but Mrs. VanderHook greeted him warmly.

"Good evening, Saidu," she said. Then, turning toward Frank, she said, "Saidu is our night watchman. He's a gift from God to us."

Lydia could see why. She couldn't believe she had to stay in this part of town. Her grandmother would be having a cow if she could see them right now.

"I hope you don't mind sleeping on couches," Mrs. VanderHook said to Lydia and her dad as she unlocked the door and stepped inside. "I don't have beds for everyone. Especially not with Cynthia here, too."

"Oh! Is she already here?" Frank asked.

"Yes, she arrived this morning. I'm sure she's sound asleep right now. Poor dear."

"Oh, don't feel sorry for Cynthia," he joked. "That woman may seem sweet, but you won't find a she-lion with more fight in her than our lovely boss."

*Great,* Lydia thought as she plunked down on the couch that was to be her bed. *Now I'm going to dream of lions again.*

But Lydia didn't dream of anything. She was hardly aware that she had even been asleep—when something suddenly woke her up.

# 5
# Not Alone

I t was pitch dark and Lydia didn't know where she was. None of the noises she heard were familiar to her. At first she thought she was at a school football game, because all she could hear was the mingling of many voices. Then she heard a strange chant, what sounded like a cross between a wolf howling and a man singing. Then she heard a snarl and scuffling right outside her window—it must have been two animals fighting.

One sound, though, she recognized: Someone was moving stealthily through the room. Lydia shook her head and remembered where she was: on a couch in the living room of the VanderHooks' house. But knowing where she was didn't make her feel any better.

She listened—and had no doubt that someone was slinking around. She couldn't imagine who it could be.

"Dad?" she whispered. The rustling stopped, and Lydia stared intently into the darkness. She could see nothing. "Who's there?" she whispered loudly.

Lydia heard the intruder slip out of the room, and then all was quiet. She lay silently for awhile—not sure if it was fear or humidity keeping her awake. She wanted to stay up and keep watch until morning, but all that traveling and the time change had made her more tired than when she had pulled an all-nighter with the youth group.

She woke up a few hours later to the sounds of morning: dishes clanging, people talking, horns honking, and roosters crowing—and the murmur of many voices that seemed to always surround the VanderHook home. She could smell fried eggs—and of course that musty smell that she knew was Africa itself.

Lydia's dad was no longer on the other couch. With sunlight streaming through the double-screened windows, Lydia could observe the VanderHooks' living room. The floor was tiled and the walls were whitewashed. The room was decorated very simply: the two couches were made from some sort of black fabric; it looked like leather but felt more like thick plastic.

A pretty wooden coffee table in the middle of the room had just a photo album and a couple of books on it. Lydia lifted the cover of the album and saw what must have been the entire VanderHook family: the three Lydia had already met plus four others who looked to be in their twenties. Maybe one couple was married. All but Ben were white. Lydia quickly closed the book.

A wooden cabinet in the corner held a small CD player and some of the wooden figurines of African women that had seemed so ugly at the airport. They looked lovely here. Above that table was a large cloth painting of an elephant.

Still wearing the same clothes as the day before, Lydia dreaded going to face a room full of people. She carefully picked out some fresh clothes—faded jeans and a Happy Bunny T-shirt—grabbed her toiletries, and began to spy around for a bathroom.

The door to the kitchen was simply an opening that gave her a view to the back door. She could hear voices, including her dad's, but no one could see her from there, so she hurried past to the staircase by the front door and tiptoed upstairs. At the top she saw two small wooden doors in front of her, one to her right and one to her left. Two more doors stood closed behind her. She turned the handle on the one closest to her—and was startled to see an older black woman sitting on a chair in front of a mirror, brushing her long hair.

The woman was wearing a long, white, cotton nightgown and wire-rimmed glasses. When she smiled in the mirror at Lydia, her teeth and the whites of her eyes beautifully contrasted with the very dark skin of her oval face. This woman was by no means thin, but the abundance of her body was somehow striking, even stately. Lydia guessed she was about sixty.

"Oh! I'm so sorry!" Lydia mumbled. "I thought—"

"It's all right, sweetheart," the woman said. Her southern accent surprised Lydia. "You must be Lydia. I'm so glad to finally meet you."

"Yes . . ." Lydia mumbled. She had no idea who the woman was.

"I'm Cynthia Bell," the woman said as she rose to shake Lydia's hand. "I'm just here for a little visit."

Visions of she-lions came immediately to mind, and Lydia smiled. Her dad had been dead wrong. This woman was far from being the vicious beast Lydia had dreamed of.

"Won't you please come in?" Mrs. Bell invited.

"Oh, I didn't mean to interrupt," Lydia said. "I was just looking for a bathroom."

"It's the door to your left. There is a bucket of warm water in the tub that you can use. I'm finished with it."

Lydia smiled as sweetly as she could and started to close the door.

"Come back this way when you're through, and we'll sneak in some girl time before we have to begin this day. I don't think I'm quite ready yet." The older woman smiled, and Lydia felt as though a majestic queen had just placed a tiara on her head.

"I will," Lydia promised.

She opened the bathroom door and turned on the light switch. It didn't work. She waited for a second until her eyes got used to the dim light coming through the small window over the tub. Through the window she could still hear the city noises. She stepped into the bathroom and closed the door. It was a tiny room but had everything she expected: a sink and mirror and toilet and tub.

She saw the white bucket in the tub as promised but wasn't quite sure what she was supposed to do with it. She tried turning on the shower, but only cold water dribbled down on her. She quickly turned it off. Finally she stepped into the bucket and began to bathe herself with a washcloth and soap. No matter how awkward this method was, Lydia was thankful to get clean.

After drying off with the towel that hung on a hook at the back of the shower, Lydia threw on her jeans and T-shirt. She tried to use her blow dryer but found that the lights weren't the only thing that didn't work. *Great, no electricity.* She put her blow dryer and curling iron away and quickly pulled her hair into one long braid. After brushing her teeth and dabbing on some lip gloss, she was already sweating. Apparently she would have to move slowly in this country to avoid dying of heat.

She knocked quietly on the bedroom door before entering. "I'm back."

Mrs. Bell had changed into a lovely dark blue and purple sundress. Her hair was pulled into a gentle bun at the nape of her neck. Lydia thought she looked more beautiful than a gemstone in the sunlight.

The bedroom had no furniture except a single bed and wooden chair. No pictures hung on the whitewashed walls. Mrs. VanderHook must have been a good seamstress though, because the bedspread was a lovely burgundy covered with tassels, and the curtains covering the screened windows matched the bedspread, just as the elegance it evoked matched the guest.

"Oh, my," Mrs. Bell said quietly, holding her hand to her chest. "I almost thought you were Nadia coming through that door!" She patted the bed. "Come sit with me."

"You knew my mother?" Lydia asked and sat down beside Mrs. Bell.

"Knew her?" the woman asked incredulously. "I practically raised her!"

"You did?" Lydia was shocked—and thrilled to meet someone who had known her mother so well.

"Well, not quite. But she came to live with me in the States as an exchange student when she was seventeen. She missed her parents in Spain, of course, but after she met your dad, there was no going back. She asked to live with me permanently, and since her sweet parents were blessing the whole situation, I agreed. I can't believe no one told you that!" Mrs. Bell put her hands on her hips. "I'm going to have to give Frankie a talking to."

Lydia laughed out loud. "I'd like to hear that."

The woman put a hand on Lydia's shoulder. "You are so much like your mother, sweetheart."

Lydia was cheesing from ear to ear. "I am? How?"

"You've got her wonderful self-possession."

"What does that mean?"

"Hmmm . . . how shall I explain it?" Mrs. Bell looked out the window. Lydia could see people everywhere, walking down the street or sitting on porches or working on cars. But she turned her attention quickly back to Mrs. Bell. "After talking to you for just a few moments," the elderly woman said, "I can already tell that you like yourself and that you like other people."

"And that's how my mom was?"

"Yes," the woman answered. "And everyone loved her back. Everyone. She had tremendous poise and she hardly knew it. She was afraid of nothing. She was selfless and passionate—my lands, I miss her."

"I do, too," Lydia said quietly.

"I can only imagine."

They were silent a moment. "It's weird," Lydia said. "Lately I've been thinking of her all the time. When I was little I sometimes forgot all about her."

"That's not surprising."

"Really? It seems like I should have missed her when I was little, not now anymore."

"Oh, I don't know. You had a lot of people looking out for you when you were small. Many people filled in the hole that your mom left. But now that you're becoming a young lady—well, no one can take the place of a mother."

"Yeah." It was weird to hear out loud the thought that had so often tumbled through her head.

"Besides, coming to Africa has to remind you of her," Mrs. Bell continued. "That's the last time you saw her, isn't it?"

"Yeah," Lydia said. "I love being here, though. Not very many people my age get to have these kinds of adventures. It's exciting!"

"I'm glad to hear that. You're a brave girl, Lydia."

*That* wasn't true, Lydia knew. "You know what? Last night I heard the strangest—"

"Lydia?" her dad called from the hallway.

"Yes, Daddy!" she called back.

"Come get some breakfast, honey."

"Okay! Coming." Lydia jumped up. "Thank you, Mrs. Bell. You're the best!"

"Call me Cynthia, please," the lady said with a kind laugh. "We're friends now."

Lydia beamed. "Hurry up and join us," she urged. "I can't wait to hear you give 'Frankie' a talking to." Lydia giggled.

"I'll be right there."

Lydia followed her dad down the stairs and into the kitchen. Like every room in the house, the walls were white and the floors were tiled. There was very little walking space around the table, single sink, tiny counter, and gas-powered fridge and stove. The back door was held open, letting in a welcome breeze. On the table was a bounty of food: slices of fresh pineapple, thick white bread, Smucker's jam, eggs fried in butter, boxes of American cereal, a glass jug of milk, coffee, tea, and cold juice.

Ben was sitting down, squished between the table and the wall, and Hink was sitting across from him. Lydia managed to squeeze in beside Ben as Mrs. VanderHook stood by the stove. "We usually have the table right up against the wall," Ben explained to Lydia. "But this is more fun."

Lydia hardly thought it was fun, so she didn't say anything. Frank glared at her. She stared back and mouthed the word "What?" If you can't say anything nice, don't say anything at all—that was what he was always telling her.

Just as the two men took a place at each head, Cynthia arrived and stood with hands on hips in the doorway to the kitchen. Her first words to Frank had nothing to do with Nadia. "A she-lion, eh?" was all she said, looking down at him from under dark brows.

Frank grinned without apology. "You heard that?" he asked.

"These old ears haven't failed me yet," she said. "A she-lion . . ." Cynthia walked toward Frank, her ample hips almost touching both the table and the counter.

Frank got up and walked around the table chuckling, and put his arms out for a hug. They embraced warmly. He kissed her on the cheek and said, "You're as beautiful as ever, Cynthia."

"Thank you, Frank. So glad to see you again."

Frank sat back down, and the three women crowded along the side opposite the kids. Dr. VanderHook led them in prayer, thanking God for the safe arrival of the guests. Lydia thought maybe God had been missing in action for a little while during all that turbulence, but kept quiet. The meal was full of laughter and conversation—except that Ben looked miserable, for whatever reason. Lydia didn't even mind that everyone laughed at her when she told them that she had stood in the bucket to take her bath.

"You're supposed to dip water from the bucket and pour it over your head, dear," Mrs. VanderHook explained. "Didn't you see the plastic cup?"

Lydia also discovered why she hadn't been able to turn on any lights—the VanderHooks used a small generator to make their own electricity, but they ran it for only a few hours every night. The rest of the time they went without. They joked about running down to Wal-Mart (as if there were any such store here) and driving on the freeway (here being on a freeway meant you were free to drive any way you wanted to), and other huge cultural differences.

Lydia was disappointed when Dr. VanderHook brought the fun to a close by saying it was time for work.

"Yeah, why put off the inevitable?" Frank said. "Show me the books, Peter, and I'll get your life all straightened out for you."

The doctor laughed. "I wish it were that easy." He turned to Lydia. "Do you want to see the clinic?" he asked.

"Sure!" she said. It would probably get her out of dish duty, anyway.

The others stayed to clean up, but Dr. VanderHook and Ben led Lydia and her dad through the living room to the door on the other side of the staircase. The couches were still covered with their stuff, but no one seemed to care.

"It's just a bit bigger than the living room, but it does the job," the doctor explained as he lifted the latch and led them into the clinic. "A reception area and two small procedure rooms. Patients wait outside—which is fine now, but it's a problem in the rainy season."

Lydia stepped in and looked politely around. She was just about to ask Dr. VanderHook a question when Ben grabbed her arm. "Lydia, this treasure hunt might be more dangerous than I thought," he whispered. "We have to talk."

"Right now?"

"Yes!"

"Dad," Lydia said, "Ben and I are going outside."

"Okay, honey," he called back.

"Come right back," Hink called from the kitchen. "We have lessons today."

"Yes, ma'am," Lydia said. She rolled her eyes at Ben as they walked out the front door. This house was most definitely too small.

People were everywhere in the yard and street—kids, men, women—and all of them black. Lydia realized that because few people owned cars here, most people walked everywhere. And being outside was more comfortable than being inside. Skinny brown dogs, all looking exactly the same to Lydia, trotted around with happy, careless expressions. The many shops looked more like the flea market stalls she had seen back home. All the buildings were banged up next to each other, and a red dust seemed to cover everything.

Yellow taxis took over most of the road where the people were not walking. All the drivers, whether in taxis or white United Nations SUVs or compact cars, seemed to be honking at each other and cutting each other off. In every direction Lydia could see soldiers or army tanks. Kids were running along the road knocking on car windows, trying to sell clean water in little plastic bags. One large truck full of soldiers drove past the kids, and a bunch of the soldiers called out to them; the kids ran alongside the truck, tossing up bags as the soldiers dropped the money down.

"Lydia, listen," Ben said. "We have a problem."

"What is it?" Lydia had to admit that her first impression of Ben had been wrong. He may not have been what she expected, but he was not shy or goofy. He had an intensity in his eyes that she had to pay attention to.

"Someone else is after the treasure," he said.

"Who?"

"I don't know. Have you told anyone about it?" he asked.

"Yes, I told my dad—"

"What?!"

"He's cool, Ben," Lydia said, feeling a little mad. "He wouldn't do anything to—"

"How can you be so sure?" Ben interrupted.

"I'm sure, okay?" she shot back.

"Okay, then, who else knows?" Ben plopped down on the front step.

"Why do you think someone else is after the treasure?" Lydia asked, sitting beside him in the morning sun. She felt like she was in a steam bath and wished she had brought sundresses rather than jeans. Ben was wearing shorts.

"My map is missing," Ben said. "And so is the first clue. I think someone came into my room last night and took it."

Lydia whistled, thinking of the intruder in the living room last night. "Oh well, it doesn't matter," she said. "We don't need it anymore."

"What do you mean?" Ben asked.

"I solved the riddle."

Ben stared at her. "And you were going to tell me about this when?"

"As soon as possible. I figured it out just last night—when we landed in Guinea."

"And?"

"Well—" Lydia looked around and saw Mrs. Hinkle looking at them from the window. Lydia gave a fake smile, and her tutor walked away. "If you unscramble the letters, it says something about peace on earth, which is exactly what the Temple of Jus—"

"The Temple of Justice says 'Let justice be done to all men,'" Ben interrupted.

"Right," Lydia continued. "That's what the clue says when it's unscrambled. So I think we have to go there."

Ben stared at her and then began scratching the clue in the sand. *JTEAM—let us ice bed on toll en.* "You're right," he said after a moment. "Let's go." He stood up.

"Right now?" He hadn't even gushed over her skills.

"Whoever took that map might be ahead of us already," Ben said. "We have to hurry."

"What about—?"

"Lydia! This is serious. If whoever took that map gets the next clue before we do, we'll never find the treasure."

"Fine," Lydia said. "How do we get there?"

"It's close. We can walk."

The word *close* means different things to different people. After walking for ten minutes along a road jammed with yellow taxis and hordes of people, Lydia started to complain: "We didn't even tell anyone what we're doing, and now we're walking halfway to America!" She didn't want to say that she also felt weird being the only white person she could see. Everyone seemed to be staring at her—or trying to sell her something.

"Don't worry," Ben said. "We're almost there." He stopped and looked around. "I think."

Lydia stared at him. "You think?" she asked. She looked at him a moment longer and then groaned loudly, putting her hands over her face. "Oh no! We're lost!"

# 6
# The Temple of Justice

W e're not lost!" Ben yelled.

"Where are we then?" Lydia asked. They were off the main road and surrounded by homes that looked just like those behind the clinic.

"I basically know where we are, but it's hard to tell neighborhoods apart. This is what all the homes look like in Monrovia, and I'm not usually off the main road."

"This is not what your place looks like," Lydia said.

"Well, that's because we live right on the main road and because . . . well, it's a clinic."

"It must be weird to have your own bedroom when your neighbors don't even have toilets," Lydia said. But when she looked at Ben, she realized she had said something wrong.

"It must be weird to be an ignorant American," he said.

"You don't have to be mean. I wasn't trying to—"

"Never mind," he said. "Sorry."

"I'm sorry, too," she mumbled. She couldn't keep up with this guy. His moods changed faster than her best friend's secret crushes. Lydia would have given anything to be back home with Amy now. "Let's just figure out how to get back to the clinic."

Without saying another word, Ben walked over to a woman who had just come out of her house. She was just a little taller than Lydia and looked to be about Frank's age. "Do you know where Sekou Toure Avenue is?" Ben asked her. "It's in Mamba Point."

"Yah," she said. "I help you."

Lydia looked more closely at the woman as she gave Ben directions. Lydia couldn't understand all of what she said, but her voice was soft and sweet. Her clothes were stylish and clean. At first she looked tired, but then she smiled. Lydia could see the woman was younger than she first thought, maybe in her early thirties.

"I show you," the woman finally said with a laugh. "You lost!"

Lydia laughed out loud. "He won't admit that, though," she said.

"No man say he be lost," the woman said with a laugh. Both kids beamed—Lydia glad to be one of the girls, and Ben . . . well, maybe Ben just liked being called a man.

"We're going to the GRO Clinic," Ben said as they walked along.

The woman glanced at him quickly and told them she knew right where it was. Lydia was already starting to understand her speech better.

They started walking, and Lydia made sure to step in beside the woman. "I'm Lydia," she said. "What's your name?"

"You don't just ask people their names, Lydia!" Ben hissed.

But the woman brushed it off. Her name was Arway, she told them, and her people were from Bomi County. She said some other things that Lydia couldn't understand but was too embarrassed to ask to have repeated. Fortunately Lydia understood Arway's last sentence: "Is your father the doctor at the clinic?"

"No, that's Ben's dad," Lydia pointed to Ben. "My dad is here for just a few weeks to . . . well, help out." Lydia didn't want to offend Ben again by saying that her dad was here to make sure everything was running smoothly. Even though he was.

"Where be your people?" Arway asked. "Dey all here?"

"Family, she means," Ben said quietly.

Lydia hated these questions. Maybe that's why you don't ask someone her name in Liberia. It leads to more questions. "Yeah. Me and my dad are the whole family. My mom died when I was little. In a plane crash."

"Your loss is great, tutu," the woman said. "Who know de way of God?"

Lydia sure didn't.

"I know dat hurt," Arway continued. "I loss my baby."

Lydia felt like she had been drilled in the chest with a basketball. "Your baby died?"

"I pray no, but I know not. Rebels rip many families apart during the war."

"She's missing?" Lydia asked, horrified.

"Yah. She been gone dees tree years. I loss her on her fift birtday," Arway said. "I pray de good Lord keep her safe."

"Why would God let her disappear in the first place?" Lydia blurted out.

Arway looked closely at Lydia. "Who know de way of God?"

Lydia didn't like that answer. "Have you tried to find her?" she asked

Arway had. She had walked to villages near and far to look at all the children. The daughter, whose name was Promise, had a birthmark—a circle about the size of a quarter—right between her eyes, so Arway knew she would recognize her still. Even now Arway's eyes were always on the children who ran by them. Many of them seemed to know her and would touch her hand in greeting. Arway would give each one a beautiful smile and some word of greeting.

"I'll help you find your daughter, Arway," Lydia said.

Arway looked at her quickly, and then shook her head. "No, tutu, I give it to God."

53

"My dad will help, too," Lydia said. "He can do anything!"

Arway thanked Lydia, but said that she had let go of that dream. She talked about the many people she had to love, about how her church had become her new family. "And I keep praying dat my baby have people to love, too."

"I pray that Promise has *you* to love!" Lydia said. It wasn't much of a prayer. She didn't believe God did anything to help mothers and daughters. But her dad would have the mystery solved by tomorrow. There was no way he'd let a mother and daughter be separated if it was in his power to prevent it.

"Lydia! Look!" Ben said. He was pointing to a building in the distance. "The Temple of Justice."

"Are you sure?" Lydia asked.

"Of course I'm sure," he said. "Let's go!"

Arway tried to direct them back to the clinic, clearly thinking of the adults who must be worried about them.

Lydia cringed. Her dad probably would be freaking out by now. They had been gone a long time. But they were so close! And it would take only a few minutes. She hugged Arway good-bye and jogged down the path beside Ben toward the main road, toward the building that sprawled in front of them, its wings spread open as if to welcome them in.

"Not there," Ben said. "That's the senate building, the capitol." He pointed a little way down the road. "There's the Temple of Justice."

Sure enough, in huge stone letters Lydia read the words that had brought them to this place: "Let justice be done to all men." Lydia had expected a palace of some sort, but this building was like a rundown apartment building in Indianapolis. Big, but not beautiful. Across the street was a massive building surrounded by huge barricades and razor wire.

"That's where the president lives. Kind of like our White House," Ben explained. "We couldn't get in there if we wanted to." He nodded toward the UN guards. "We're not even allowed to take pictures." He pointed to a sign that illustrated an X-ed out camera.

But when they walked up the path toward the Temple of Justice, the Liberian guards in front merely nodded at them.

"Did you know this country used to be like a little America?" Ben asked as they both looked at the flag waving over them. With eleven red and white stripes and one white star in a blue field at the upper inside corner, the Liberian flag looked a lot like the American flag. Lydia had actually thought it was the US flag at first.

"What do you mean?" Lydia asked, unbelieving. This place was a pit.

"Well, Liberia was founded by a bunch of freed American slaves. Monrovia is named after the American president Monroe. Things were very good here for a long time. Very modern.'"

"Modern?" Lydia looked around. Yeah. She could see it. If she looked hard. She could see some windows that might have been stained glass before they were shot out. It might have been beautiful once. "Charles Taylor did all this?"

"Yeah. He went from being a corrupt rebel to being a corrupt president. His men destroyed everything. Just for fun. Roads. Electricity. Wells. People. Everything."

"Ugh. How long ago was he prez?"

"Not long," Ben said. "Just before we got here he was arrested. The new president didn't come into office until 2006. Anyway, that's why everyone speaks English."

"Yeah, I was surprised that Arway spoke English. But it was hard to understand her sometimes."

"Yeah, they have strong accents. And Liberian English is different anyway. They change the order of the words around and pronounce them different and sometimes add new ones. But most of them speak American English, too."

They stood in front of the building, staring up at the huge stone letters imprinted into the wall. The guards wandered nearby but didn't stop them.

"I guess that means we're allowed in here," Ben whispered.

Lydia gasped. "This is your first time here?"

"Yeah. Remember, the civil war just ended. We never could have done this before. Charles Taylor would have had us scalped."

"He would?"

"No!" Ben laughed. "Whoa, you're jumpy! I don't know what he would have done. I never tried to find out."

"So, what do we do now?" Lydia asked.

"I don't know. You're the one who said we needed to come here."

"Right." Lydia straightened her shoulders and looked around. "We have to find the next clue."

"Clue?" Ben asked.

"Yes, we're clearly on a treasure hunt. The person who set this thing up is not going to send us straight to the treasure."

"Oh, yeah."

"You don't happen to have the original clue with you, do you?" She had never even seen the first clue. Ben had only told her the scrambled letters.

"It was stolen, remember?"

"Rats. It seems like it would have had some mark on there to show us where the next clue would be hidden."

"Well," Ben said, "let's start looking." He began poking around the ground under the stone letters on the wall. "It's got to be here somewhere."

After a half hour of looking Lydia gave up. "It's just not here, Ben," she said, plunking down on the dirt. "The other person must have gotten here first."

Ben squatted down beside her. "Umm," he said, "you'd better not sit down. There are lots of red ants around here."

Lydia jumped up, and hit her hand on the wall as she did. "Oww!" she yowled as she hopped around sucking her knuckle, which had started to bleed. "I should have just let the ants get me!"

Ben wasn't looking at her, though. "Lydia," he said quietly.

When she finally looked at him, Lydia stopped hopping. Her mouth opened, and a million red ants might have crawled inside as she stood there staring. "We found it," she said. When her hand had hit the wall the letter N must have been jarred, and now they could easily see the corner of a small plastic bag poking out from under it. Lydia reached up to pull it out, and they could see a folded note inside.

"Hey, kids," a soldier called. "You've been hanging out here too long. Move on."

Lydia's heart was beating as fast as a baby bird's, but she looked up and smiled sweetly. "Sure," she said. "We were just going." She stuck the bag in her jeans pocket and walked down the path toward the gate, Ben walking stride for stride beside her.

They didn't say anything until they were out of the soldiers' sight. Suddenly Ben turned to Lydia and grinned. He pulled her into a hug.

She felt her face burning, but laughed anyway. "You're crazy."

"No, I'm not!" he said. "That's just it. I thought I was crazy for thinking this treasure hunt was real, but I'm not. It *is* real! Let's look at the next clue."

# 7
# The Dad Factor

They didn't get a chance to read the clue. Dr. VanderHook's Pathfinder pulled up beside them, and Frank bellowed at them to get in. He seemed to be too stressed out to say anything, and Lydia knew she was in big trouble.

She could see people through the window of the VanderHooks' house walking toward the front door when they pulled up. A crowd of people loitered outside the clinic doors.

Lydia scooted out of the car, and Ben whispered in her ear. "We might get grounded. But no matter what happens, we read that clue together. Got it?"

"Right!" She patted her pocket where the clue was safely hidden.

"Where were you?" Mrs. VanderHook demanded as she stepped out of the house with Cynthia and Hink close behind her. Her face couldn't have been more screwed up if someone had twisted her nose 360 degrees.

"You can't just disappear like that!" Hink said crossly. "You have to communicate." She said the last word slowly, as if they couldn't understand her.

"Sorry," Ben said.

"My lands, you scared us!" Cynthia said.

"That's for sure!" Frank said angrily, slamming the door behind him. "We have enough concerns without having to worry about you!"

"Dad," Lydia said, "we met this woman whose daughter went missing. It's so sad! We just have to help her, Daddy—"

But "Daddy" was in no mood to help. He made it clear that his own missing daughter was in big trouble, and that he wasn't about to talk about other issues until this one was resolved. Lydia knew better than to talk back. The conversation was short.

"I think the two of you can work in the clinic for the rest of the day," Dr. VanderHook said. "We've got plenty to keep you busy—and out of trouble."

"Great idea, Pete," Mrs. VanderHook said.

"Well, I've got to get back to work," Dr. VanderHook said.

"So do I," Dad said, still fuming. "Come on."

The little group walked toward the crowd, and Lydia felt like everyone was looking at them. Young and old, the waiting patients sat on ledges or squatted on the ground or lounged on the few lawn chairs set out by the door. Like a group of teenagers at the park on a hot summer day back in Indiana, nobody was moving much, except maybe to swat a fly. Dr. VanderHook went straight in, smiling kindly at the folks who greeted him.

"Can we eat lunch before we start working, Mom?" Ben asked quietly, careful to not let any patients hear.

"Fine."

Frank went into the clinic where Dr. VanderHook was—with the promise of coming back to address this with Lydia later—while the rest of the group went through the house door to the kitchen. Mrs. VanderHook nagged Ben for about ten minutes about responsibility, and Lydia just stared at the floor the entire time. She was in shock. Her dad was supposed to be able to do anything—but he was clearly uninterested in helping.

Finally Mrs. VanderHook told the kids to sit down. She served them a big bowl of soup and rice, a peanut butter sandwich, and a couple of chocolate chip cookies, topped off by a large glass of cold juice from the gas-powered fridge. Mrs. Bell—*Cynthia*—joined them at the table. Then Hink came and sat down, too.

"I'm glad you're here," Ben said, as if nothing big had just happened. "Mom hardly ever buys American food."

"It's too expensive," Mrs. VanderHook said. "We only buy it for special occasions."

Lydia hadn't realized how hungry she was. It was well past noon, and she hadn't eaten a thing since breakfast.

"Those people waiting outside probably haven't eaten this much all week," Ben said. "They probably eat only rice and soup once a day." He didn't sound mad or anything—just amazed. Like he couldn't imagine living without his mom's good cooking himself and he didn't know how others did it.

Lydia supposed they didn't. Many people died of starvation in Africa. But was that true even here in Monrovia? "Why are they here?" Lydia asked. "What's wrong with them? Do they just need nutrition?" She started to feel bad about enjoying her soup so much. Maybe she should have given some to one of the patients.

"They do," Cynthia said, "but Dr. VanderHook mainly treats AIDS patients."

Lydia stiffened. She had been right in the middle of that crowd. "Isn't that contagious?"

"Relax," Hink said. "You don't get AIDS the same way you get a cold."

"How do you get it?"

"By having *sex* with someone who has it!" Ben said.

He didn't sound embarrassed, but Lydia giggled.

"It's not funny," he said. "People can also get AIDS if they're exposed to contaminated body fluids, including blood, like on a needle that an infected person has used for drugs."

He sounded like a doctor.

"Actually, it sometimes scares me," Ben said as he took a bite of his peanut butter sandwich, "because my dad is always dealing with their blood. He'd just better be careful, that's all I can say."

"Amen to that," Mrs. VanderHook said. She got up and started clearing the dishes. Hink got up to help her.

"Your dad is to be admired for his willingness to take risks in this job," Cynthia said, "but I can assure you that he is very careful, Ben."

Ben just looked at her.

"I know this because I am an RN who has worked beside him many times," Cynthia said in response to his unasked question. "Docs don't come any better than him."

Ben smiled. For real. Cynthia's words must have meant a lot to him.

If only Cynthia could say something to Lydia to make her feel better about *her* dad. She didn't need reminding that he was able to do nearly anything—she just needed to figure out why he wouldn't do it. All she asked was that he help her find this one little girl. It wasn't like he was doing much here anyway.

Cynthia got up to help the other women. They finished their work and then went out the back door to admire Mrs. VanderHook's garden.

"Let's read the clue!" Lydia said the second the women were out of earshot.

"Yes!" Ben said. "Quick! Give it to me."

"No," Lydia said. "I'll read it."

"I get to! It's my treasure hunt," Ben said.

Lydia glared at him. "Do you want me to help you find this hidden treasure or not?"

"I don't care," he said. "Now give it."

"Well, then, you shouldn't have told me about it in the first place. I'm in this with you, and I'm reading the clue. I'm older than you."

Lydia pulled out the note and began unfolding it. Ben tried to snatch it away.

"Let go!" Lydia yelled. "Do you want to rip it?"

"What's going on in here?" Hink said as she came into the house.

"Nothing," both kids responded. Lydia quickly let go of the note and Ben pulled it under the table.

"Hmmm," the old lady said. She leaned against the door-frame. Not moving. "What do you have there?"

"Nothing," Ben said.

"Come on," Hink said, moving toward the kids. "Give it up."

"Mrs. Hinkle!" Lydia begged. "Please just leave it!"

But the tutor seemed only more firm. She held out her hand.

"Okay . . ." Ben said as he pulled his hand up from under the table.

"No, Ben—" Lydia began . . . until she heard Hink scream as she stared at the dung beetle Ben had dropped in her hand.

The woman flung the bug across the room and continued to shake her hand long after it had fallen from its perch.

Lydia didn't show her surprise for long. She quickly got into the game. "Ben! You let it get away!"

He scrambled onto the floor and searched around for the critter so desperately that Lydia almost believed him herself. She saw him slip the clue into his pocket as she joined him in the search. Lucky for both of them, the bug had vanished.

Hink hadn't, though.

"I know your type," she said to the kids. "Your parents may think you're perfect little angels, but I know better." She walked back outside.

"That was amazing, Ben!" Lydia said. "You're my new hero!"

He smiled. "It just worked out," he said.

Lydia didn't feel bad at all about the little prank—but she soon would.

A drop of sweat fell from Lydia's nose onto her bare arm.

"I think you kids have worked hard enough," Dr. VanderHook said, as he admired their work. "I hoped you learned your lesson."

Lydia squirmed. She really should have learned her lesson by now. Besides being forced to organize supplies in the back room of the clinic for the last three hours—under Hink's unmerciful supervision—she had endured the longest lecture ever from her dad. As he went on and on about how much she scared him, even to the point of crying, Lydia remembered her cat back in Indiana after its kittens were taken away. For weeks that cat had wandered around the house looking for them. Lydia felt like a worm-infested apple for making her dad feel that way.

But Arway's little girl, Promise, was still missing, and he wasn't going to do a thing about it. When she had tried to talk to him about it again, he practically yelled at her. "You're missing the point, Lydia!" he said. "You're missing the point."

"It looks like Mrs. Hinkle is ready to start lessons," Dr. VanderHook said.

Lessons? Now? It was suppertime! Lydia looked over at Hink, who had not even once allowed the kids to take a break. She had been preparing lessons the last few hours, and her bony rump must have been hurting in that small wooden chair. She was probably coming up with all kinds of terrible ways to torment them. They were to begin their three-week crash course in algebra. Lydia had never studied algebra before, and it sounded scary. Especially now that she saw the little smirk on her teacher's face.

"Let's go, children," Hink said, too sweetly.

Lydia groaned and followed Hink. At least they were in it together—Ben was to "take advantage" of having such an excellent teacher around. Ben had whispered earlier to Lydia that he thought his mom just wanted a break from homeschooling him.

It was as bad as Lydia thought it would be. She hated math. Who cared what x was? Unless it was marking the spot on a treasure map. But the lesson ended sooner than expected because Mrs. VanderHook, for all her nagging, was really a softy. She didn't think the children should be made to suffer too long. "After all, it is past seven," she said to Lydia's dad. "They need their dinner."

Their teacher seemed reluctant to give them up, but once they were all sitting at the table stuffing their faces with cassava-leaf soup and fried fish, plus frozen pineapple chunks for dessert, even Hink was laughing (snorting, actually) at the crazy jokes her dad was telling. He did tell funny stories, Lydia had to admit, but she was still mad at him.

"Dad," she said after dinner, "do we have to do school tomorrow?"

"Of course y—" he started to say.

"Dad! I just got here. I want to explore."

"Well, after this afternoon I don't—"

"This afternoon was because—" Lydia cut in.

"Don't interrupt me, Lydia," her dad said softly.

Lydia sighed.

"Anyway, we went through that already." He paused. "Here's the deal: You do have to do a couple hours of schoolwork with Mrs. Hinkle in the morning," he said. "And then, if you promise to be careful, you may go exploring, but—"

"Yes! We'll be care—"

"Ahem," her dad said. "What did I tell you about interrupting?"

"Sorry," Lydia quickly said.

"As I was saying," continued her dad, "you may go exploring with Ben, but he's in charge. You may be older, but he knows this area. Do you promise to listen to him?"

Lydia slumped her shoulders. "Yes."

Ben laughed as they ran up the stairs to his room where they would finally be able to read the clue. "I'm the boss," he said proudly.

Lydia just groaned. "I'm going to kill my dad!"

They left the bedroom door open (because that was the dumb rule) and shared Ben's desk chair as they *finally* read the clue together. They unrolled the folded paper note and put it under Ben's lamp.

## Find Big Henry. Trust God.

That's all it said.

"Big Henry," Lydia said. "Is that a restaurant?"

"I don't know," Ben answered. "It could be a person."

"He'd be ancient by now," Lydia said. "I wonder how old these clues are."

"I think about ten years. Remember the people at the post office said the mail had been there for about that long."

"Let's destroy the clue," Lydia said. "I don't want anyone else to find it."

"Good idea," Ben said. "Let's flush it down the toilet."

"Wait!" Lydia said. "Let's burn it. That way we'll be sure."

"Okay, let's go get some matches." Ben got up. He stuffed the clue in his desk drawer for now.

Lydia stood up and said, "I'm going to find Arway tomorrow."

"What?" Ben said. He turned around to stare at her. "Why?"

"I *have* to. I want to help her find her daughter."

"Did you ask your dad?" Ben asked.

"I'm too mad at him for not even pretending to care about this," Lydia said. "Besides, he'd never let me go talk to a stranger."

Ben sat down. "Don't you think he has a point?"

"No!" Lydia said. "You talked to her first. You can see she's good!"

"Yes, but—"

"I'm doing this," Lydia said. "Please keep it a secret. This is important to me." She leaned all the way over to him and grabbed his wrist. "Please, Ben."

"Fine," he said quietly.

"Promise?" she asked.

"Okay," he said. "I promise."

# 8
## Hink Stink

The next morning—Tuesday—they could hardly concentrate while Hink tried to make numbers interesting to them. Once when Ben grumbled about how useless this was, their teacher said, "Think of it as a treasure hunt."

"What?" Ben said, his head popping up from his arms.

"A puzzle," Hink continued, apparently unaware of how her words had affected them. "A mystery to solve."

"What are you trying to say?" Lydia asked.

"Okay, try this," Hink said. "It's like your computer games: You keep playing and playing until you finally beat the level, right?" The kids nodded. "Think of algebra that same way. Keep thinking it through until you master it. It's fun!"

Fun?

Whatever.

And Hink had just made a big mistake. Lydia now knew without a doubt who their enemy was. Somehow Gretchen Hinkle (or whoever she really was!) had found out about the treasure. Well, there was no way she'd beat them to the finish line. Lydia would make sure of that.

They stuck with math at the kitchen table for another hour until finally they were dismissed. They jumped up in a hurry.

"Where are you going?" Hink asked.

"Out," Ben said.

"For some exploring?" Hink asked.

"Kind of," Lydia said.

"How nice," the teacher said, clearly considering it to be as "nice" as a broken fingernail. But then she stood up and started stretching in her typical exaggerated style. "I think I'll do the same myself now that I have the afternoon off." She looked them right in the eyes, pulled a brown bag out of the fridge, and walked out of the room.

Lydia and Ben looked at each other and shrugged. The woman was up to no good, but what could they do to stop her?

They made some sandwiches and shoved them into their backpacks as quickly as possible. Not only did they want maximum time to "explore," they wanted to get away from Hink. The last thing they needed was for her to follow them.

"Let's go find Arway," Lydia said the moment they were out of earshot.

"Arway?" Ben asked. "Now?"

"We have to get more information about her daughter."

"I thought we were looking for Big Henry."

"Ben!" Lydia said. "What's more important? A treasure or a girl?"

"Ummm . . ."

"Ben!"

"Okay—the girl. But I don't think we should be the ones to look for her. We're just kids."

"Kids can make a difference! In Brussels I saw a statue of a little boy who peed on explosives that were going to blow up the city. He's now a hero." Ben laughed, but Lydia kept talking. "Or think of Anne Frank!" she continued. "She sure made a difference in the world!"

"Yeah," Ben said, "but we can't be stupid."

"Right," Lydia said. "We'll be smart. We'd better get going."

Ben groaned as he jogged to catch up to her. "So much for me being the boss."

"Well," Lydia said, "what would you do?"

Ben shrugged and kept walking.

Before they got to Arway's neighborhood, Lydia spotted a YMCA sign. "Hey!" she said. "Let's go in there and see if they can help."

Ben seemed glad to do that.

They walked into the YMCA building, which looked as run down as any other building in the area, but it was cool inside. Apparently they kept their generator running during the day. The receptionist looked to be in her early twenties and was wearing tight jeans with leather lacing down the sides and a bright red blouse to match her lipstick. Lydia thought she was very pretty. "Can I help you?" she asked in a Liberian accent.

"Umm. Yes," Lydia said. "Do you do any work to try to reunite lost kids with their families?"

The woman said that the YMCA didn't do that, but she offered to introduce them to one of the other staff members who worked with youth.

"Okay," Lydia said.

The youth worker, Lemuel, was a handsome black guy who had grown up in Liberia, gone to college in the UK, and had just come back to Monrovia a year ago to serve the community. Within a few minutes, before they even knew his name, he had Lydia and Ben cracking up.

"You're so lucky you don't have to sit in a classroom for school," Lemuel said after they told him a bit about themselves.

"When I was in third grade, I sneezed and bumped my face on my desk." He demonstrated a sneeze that sent his head hurtling into his outspread hand. "My friends started snickering, and soon even the teacher heard about it. Class had to be canceled that day because no one could stop laughing."

Lydia laughed so hard she almost forgot why she was there as this comedian carried on.

"So," Lemuel finally said, "what can I do for you?"

Lydia went straight to business. "Do you know how I can help a mother find her daughter who was lost during the war?"

Lemuel whistled between his teeth. "You don't ask for much, do you?"

"It's very important to me," Lydia said.

"I can imagine," he said. But Lemuel really didn't have much to offer. Apparently this sort of situation was common around there. Many, many children had been orphaned or lost during the war.

They chatted a while longer, but finally even Lydia had to admit this was a dead end. They thanked him for his time and stood up.

"Hey," Ben said as they walked out the door, "have you ever heard of Big Henry?"

"Is that a candy bar?" the man asked.

"I think it's a person," Ben said. "But don't worry about it."

"Wait," Lemuel said. "You don't mean that rebel leader, do you?"

"A rebel leader!" Ben exclaimed, obviously shocked. "We were thinking this guy would be a preacher or something."

Lemuel laughed. "Well, perhaps they need a preacher on Water Street, but this chap isn't it."

"Water Street?" Lydia asked.

"It's a tough neighborhood not far away," Lemuel said. "We get a lot of our students from there."

"Students?" Lydia asked. "I thought this was a Y."

"Oh, you wagered we'd be an athletic center," he said. "No, that's more often in America. Here we provide education and counsel for kids who have been involved in or hurt by the war—things like that."

"Wow. Very cool," Lydia said. "But do you at least have a swimming pool?"

Lemuel laughed again. "No, we don't."

Someone walked in the door behind them and Lemuel turned his attention away from them. Lydia turned around—and saw Hink walking into the building. The tutor looked surprised to see them, but Lydia knew better. She must have been following them.

After briefly greeting the kids, Hink turned her attention to the two adults. "I'm helping out at the GRO Clinic," she said, "and I've been asked to deliver a gift to the new director, welcoming him into the area and letting him know a bit about our clinic." She sounded very nice. Weird.

"She's probably lying," Ben whispered as they walked out.

"Well, we'd just better get to Water Street before she does!" Lydia said.

"And look for a rebel soldier? Are you crazy?" Ben asked.

"The war is over," Lydia said.

"Yeah, but Big Henry may not think so."

"Ben, we have to!" Lydia said.

"I thought you wanted to go find Arway," Ben said.

Lydia scrunched up her nose. He was right. "Grr! Now what?" she asked.

"Let's find Arway," Ben said as he started to walk. "I don't mind saying I'm scared to death of rebels. I don't want to go there."

Lydia didn't say anything for a moment as they walked on. Then she grabbed Ben's arm. "What did the clue say?" Lydia asked.

"Find Big Henry."

"What else?" Lydia prompted.

Ben hesitated. "Trust God," he finally said.

"Right," Lydia said. Trusting God wasn't exactly her strong suit, but she was ready to start trying if that's what it took. "If we trusted God, we'd go to Water Street," she said.

Ben stared at her for a moment, but then his shoulders slumped. "Fine," he said. "But I've got to go to the bathroom first."

"Now?"

"Duh." Ben turned around.

"Where are you going?" Lydia demanded.

"Back to the Y. I've got to go."

"Fine. But we're going to Water Street afterward."

"Fine."

Back at the Y, the lady smiled at them. "Back already?"

"We just have to use the bathroom," Lydia said. "Is that okay?"

The lady pointed out the way. Lydia finished before Ben and waited outside. He took forever.

"Okay," she said when he finally came outside. "Are you ready?" She didn't blame him for being nervous. She actually was, too.

"It's this way," he said. "Come on."

A few minutes later they stopped to eat their sandwiches, even though it wasn't close to lunchtime. Ben had suddenly become starving. Lydia wanted to buy some water but resisted because she had a limited amount of cash that her dad had given her for this trip. He had given her two thousand Liberian dollars, which was almost forty American dollars, to last the entire time. She could use her own American money, of course, but the Liberian money went further.

As they sat watching the cars and people all trying to have their space on the dirt road, they spotted Dr. VanderHook's Pathfinder approaching them, moving the same direction they were. From the driver's seat Hink smiled and waved at them as she passed.

"She'd better not be going where I think she's going!" Ben said as Lydia held up her hand in a surprised wave.

"Come on!" Lydia said.

They shoved the half-eaten sandwiches into the backpack and started jogging.

# 9
# Diamonds Are Forever

**B**ut Water Street wasn't as scary as they thought it would be. It was certainly a crowded area—even more crowded than the typical packed street—but most people hardly even looked at them. Well, except for the kids. The kids didn't listen to their questions, though (maybe they didn't understand American English); they just held out their hands for money.

"Do you know who Big Henry is?" Ben kept asking in every language he knew.

The people only walked away.

"I'm tired," Lydia said. Exhausted was more like it. She could have curled up on the side of the road and fallen asleep even though it was only like two in the afternoon. The only thing that would be better than a nap would be a bucket of water dumped on her head.

Or a gray Pathfinder driving toward them.

"Mrs. Hink—!" Lydia started to yell as the car approached. The car slowed down and Lydia saw Cynthia Bell behind the wheel.

"Hop in, kids," she said.

They did thankfully.

"What in the world are you doing here?" Cynthia asked as she handed them each a bottle of water.

"Exploring," Ben said quietly, looking at the floor.

Lydia knew it was easier to lie to someone she didn't know than to someone she respected. She wondered if Ben felt guilty.

Cynthia harrumphed. Lydia fully expected a lecture to come soon.

They drove for a few minutes in silence until they came to the ocean. The dirt and noise and commotion of the city fell away, and a gorgeous sandy beach with waving palm trees opened up in front of them. "We were this close to the ocean?" Lydia asked, forgetting the trouble they were in for a moment.

"The whole time," Cynthia said, parking the car. "Come on. Let's walk on the beach."

The blue water rolled endlessly and the wind blew through Lydia's hair. She felt cool for the first time since she had arrived in Africa. "It's beautiful!" Lydia said. She took off her shoes in the white sand. "Can I go in?" she called, running toward the water.

"If you want to be shark food," Ben yelled back.

Lydia stopped in her tracks.

"I doubt the sharks would get you," Cynthia said as she came up beside Lydia, "but let's just enjoy the view for now."

They sat down and listened to the waves lapping against the shore. Cynthia was quiet for a moment. "What's going on, guys?" she finally said. She looked them both in the face, one at a time.

Lydia glanced at Ben—*Should we tell?*

He nodded.

"We're on a treasure hunt," Lydia said. It sounded silly to say it out loud to someone as refined as Cynthia.

Cynthia didn't flinch. "What kind of treasure?" she asked.

"We don't know for sure, but we think diamonds," Ben said quietly.

"Is that what brought you to Water Street?" Cynthia asked.

The kids nodded.

"Do you realize how unsafe that area is?" Cynthia directed the question to Ben.

Ben nodded again, but Lydia cut in. "It was my idea," she said miserably. "Ben knew we shouldn't."

Cynthia turned her eyes to Lydia. "Didn't your dad say that Ben was boss?" she asked.

Lydia remembered what her dad said about Cynthia being a lion. "Yes, but—"

Cynthia held up her finger and Lydia fell quiet. "Honestly, I think it's rather exciting that you're hunting for a treasure," Cynthia said. "Just be careful. Water Street is not safe."

"We were just trying to trust God!" Lydia said.

Cynthia stared at her as if she couldn't believe what Lydia had said. "Trust God? Do you think trusting God is about doing whatever you want and expecting Him to cover for you?"

Lydia didn't know what to say. She hadn't exactly thought about it.

"Trusting God is believing that He knows what is best. It's believing that He is good. It's going wherever *He* takes you—not the other way around."

What Cynthia said made sense.

But what if He didn't know what was best? What if He wasn't good?

"Besides," Cynthia said, "getting caught up in the dream of too much money—"

"It's not for us!" Ben cut in. "We would use it for the clinic. Imagine how a million dollars' worth of diamonds would help my dad!"

"Yes," Cynthia said. "But don't let the pursuit of a treasure interfere with the work that needs to be done. Now," she continued, looking at Lydia, "what else?"

Lydia took a breath. "Well, we met this lady whose daughter got stolen from her, and I promised I would help find her. I told Dad about it, and he doesn't seem to care." She looked at Ben and Cynthia in exasperation, but they didn't react. "So, I need to go talk to her."

"Thank you for telling me," Cynthia said.

"I know she's a stranger," Lydia continued in a rush, "but this woman is brokenhearted, Cynthia." Lydia choked on her words. "She misses her daughter so much. I have to do something!"

"And we shall do something," Cynthia said. "We'll start with prayer."

Lydia groaned.

"What?" Cynthia asked. "You don't want to pray about it?"

"Well, I want to pray, but that's not really helping," Lydia said. "Praying is what you do when you know you can't do anything else. First I want to *do* something."

Cynthia raised her eyebrows just a bit. "You and I think about prayer a little differently. When I pray, I know that God is listening. And He knows a whole lot more than I do. I'd rather start with Him than wear myself out with my own plans."

Lydia grunted.

"What is it?" Cynthia asked.

"I just wish my dad would help."

"With finding this little girl?"

"Yes!" Lydia said. "He didn't even care when I told him about it. And I know he would be able to figure it out if he tried."

"As much as I respect your dad, Lydia," Cynthia said, "I don't trust him to accomplish the impossible. Only God can do that."

Lydia sighed and looked back down. "So you think it's impossible to find that girl?"

"By our own power, yes," Cynthia said. "This whole country is full of displaced families. Lydia, let's pray, okay?"

Lydia sniffed. "Okay." Lydia had never met anyone she admired more than Cynthia. Maybe she was right. Maybe.

"You too, Ben," Cynthia said.

They all bowed their heads and closed their eyes as the heat of the sun warmed them and the sound of the waves comforted them. Cynthia kept silent for several minutes. Lydia was glad, because the anger she had been directing toward her dad suddenly flowed toward God. *Why won't You do anything for Promise and Arway—or for me and my mom?* For the first time ever Lydia was addressing God for real. She wasn't just reciting a prayer.

"Dear Lord Jesus," Cynthia began quietly, "I pray that You will fill us with Your Spirit so that we may have faith."

Lydia's eyes were squeezed shut, but her tears found a way out. Without words, she confessed to God her fear for Arway, her sorrow over her mother, and her willingness to give all this anguish to Him. It was like her prayer was liquid God could hold in His hands, and Lydia could almost feel His gentle smile as He eagerly accepted it from her.

"We ask You for the impossible," Cynthia said. "We pray that You will help this little girl and her mother find each other again. Use us, if You will. We love You. Amen."

"Amen," Ben said.

Lydia didn't say anything. She had too many emotions tumbling around inside her. Relief. And joy. And excitement. Plus a little bit of fear. She had finally met God.

*I trust You, Lord,* her heart whispered. *I want so much for Arway to find Promise, but maybe it's just because I want my mom back so much. I'll quit trying to make things go the way I want them to. You know best. I just pray that You will do what is right. And that You'll let us all feel okay with whatever You decide.*

Lydia stuck her fingers deep into the sand. It was going to be okay. Cynthia was right. God could reunite Arway and Promise if He wanted to. It was up to Him.

Lydia's fingers touched something hard and cold. She pulled it up to see if she had unearthed a shell. Rather than admiring a little gray clamshell, she found herself staring at a gold ring encasing a large, heart-shaped diamond.

Lydia closed her fist around the ring and sucked in her breath. If she thought her heart had been beating like a baby bird's when they'd found the second clue at the Temple of Justice, now it must've been beating like a baby bird's after running a marathon!

The weird thing was that Lydia didn't have the type of elation she would get on Christmas morning when her dad bought exactly the right gifts for her and she just had to call her best friend Amy to describe every outfit and gadget in detail. This time her excitement felt more like it did after she performed the lead role of the school play . . . flawlessly. She didn't want to talk about it with anyone. She just wanted to savor the moment.

Lydia knew she should tell the others about her find—this thing must be worth at least a couple hundred dollars—but Lydia closed her eyes and kept silent as the significance of her discovery moved deeper into her heart. She would tell them later. For now she needed to enjoy the thrill of learning how to pray and seeing the immediate and beautiful answer from God. *God, You are amazing!* Lydia prayed. Lydia's mother had not been able to give her the heirloom—a heart-shaped diamond just like this one—but God could. And He did!

Lydia opened her eyes and realized she was still crying.

She laughed and stood up, brushing her tears away. "All right," she said. "I won't talk to Arway alone. And I won't go back to Water Street alone. That was crazy thinking."

"Amen!" Ben said.

Lydia kicked sand at him. But she was too happy to care much about his teasing.

"Let's keep praying," Cynthia said. "And meanwhile I'll do some snooping around to see what I can find out."

As Lydia gave Cynthia all the details that she knew about the missing girl, she fingered the jewel in her hand. God most definitely could reunite Arway and Promise. Lydia just hoped he would.

On the way home, Cynthia told the kids about her first trip to Africa when she'd been just nine years old. She had gotten separated from her parents and a kind African family took her in for about a week before she was reunited with her mom and dad. Ever since then she had been in love with the idea of meeting folks all over the world. "There are so many wonderful people hidden away in all corners," she said. "I wish I could meet them all."

"It sounds like you've met quite a few," Lydia said.

"Yes, that's true," Cynthia said. "Actually, I'm heading out to Haiti tomorrow to meet some more."

"You are?" Lydia cried. "But I don't want you to leave."

Cynthia smiled. "We'll stay in touch. Now that I know you, I'm not letting you go. I'm practically your grandmother, after all."

"So that means I can call you so you can tell me how to figure out all my problems?" Lydia asked.

"Is that what grandmas do?" Cynthia said with a laugh. "Yes, Lyddy, call me anytime. I would be so happy to hear from you."

"You're not going to tell my dad where you found us, are you?" Lydia asked. "I really truly have learned my lesson this time."

"I won't tell," Cynthia said, "if you promise me you won't go off gallivanting without an adult."

"I promise!" Lydia said. And she meant it.

Back at the clinic, Lydia and Ben talked about how to find Big Henry without being stupid. Lydia still held on to the diamond ring.

"I'm not worried about it anymore," Lydia said. "It'll all work out."

"I sure hope so," Ben said. "If we really find this treasure, just think of what we can do with it!"

Lydia didn't need to be reminded. She would be able to launch an all-out search for Promise! It would be so exciting! She'd probably also get a laptop for herself. And maybe update her iPod. Not to mention shopping at the mall anytime she—

Ben's voice broke into her thoughts. "We could build a new clinic and actually hire some nurses and maybe even get a supply of medicine. My dad wouldn't be so worn out, and way more people could get help. Just think!"

Lydia blushed, ashamed of her own selfishness compared to Ben's generosity. "Yeah," she said quietly. "That money really could make a difference here." She thought of Arway and how a little cash would have made all the difference to her. She could have bought a little car or a plane ticket and traveled someplace farther than her feet could take her to search for her daughter.

For a moment she wondered if she should give up her diamond to help fund the search for Promise. Quickly, though, she put that idea out of her mind. This diamond was God's gift to her. How could she just give it away?

But she needed some way to help Arway.

"Ben," she said with conviction, putting away all thoughts of laptops and iPods, "we have to find that treasure."

"I know," he said, just as earnestly. "And soon."

"Maybe we can just go to the beach and see if there are diamonds in the sand there," she said. It was lame, she knew, but she still didn't want to share her secret—now not only because she wanted to hold on to the special memory, but because she wanted to hold on to the ring. Ben would probably try to talk her into giving it up.

"That's just crazy," Ben said. "Why would we do that?"

Lydia shrugged and went back to brainstorming ways to find Big Henry while still keeping their commitment to be safe. All they came up with was a headache.

Wednesday morning everyone but the two dads went to the airport to see Cynthia off. Lydia would have preferred the company of Cynthia in the backseat with her and Ben, but Hink's smaller size made that arrangement more practical.

Hink sat behind the driver's seat, opened the window a crack, and stuck all her fingers into the open space. "I like the fresh air," she said to Lydia.

Lydia was squished in the middle seat—but at least she could see out the front window. They slowed down and came to a stop at the checkpoint. Lydia sat forward in her seat to see better. The checkpoint was simply a stack of sandbags blocking their side of the road and a stack of sandbags blocking the other side of the road a few yards farther. A soldier with a machine gun just waved them through, and Mrs. VanderHook went around the sandbags and past the soldiers holding traffic on the other side.

"Our license plate has 'NGO' on it," she explained as she picked up speed, "so these checkpoints are not usually a problem. The UN soldiers have been instructed to leave NGOs alone—"

"What are NGOs?" Lydia asked.

"Non-government organizations. There are many in Monrovia doing things like providing medical care, rebuilding roads, providing relief services, starting businesses. Things like that. The government is so busy just trying to establish order they don't have the resources to provide services like that. They depend on the NGOs."

Lydia soon got used to stopping at checkpoints every few miles and hardly even noticed the soldiers and tanks. She was also experienced enough to bring her own water from the VanderHooks' filtered tank so she wouldn't have to buy the expensive packaged water. She had even remembered to carry small Liberian bills so she could buy trinkets from vendors.

What Lydia hadn't yet adapted to was the waiting. The plane was scheduled to leave at two-thirty, so they had arrived at noon. They sat outside in the waiting area where a bunch of hard benches had been set up on a concrete slab under a makeshift roof. They were out from under the hot sun, but Lydia was still dying of heat. For four hours! The plane didn't even arrive at the airport until five, and Cynthia didn't get to check in until one hour before that.

During the wait, Lydia spent as much time at Cynthia's side as she could. They browsed through boxes of homemade jewelry and examined each tie-dyed shirt presented to them. She was even tempted by those wooden figurines she had once thought so ugly—curios, they were called. If she could have found a curio of a kid with a backpack on his head, she would have bought that for sure. It cracked her up every time she saw someone carrying a backpack that way. What did they think the straps were for?

She ended up giving all the money she had to a girl whose hands had been severed, probably by rebels during the war, and wished she had brought more.

When it was time for Cynthia to leave, Lydia jumped up for a hug goodbye. "You promise to keep in touch?" Lydia said when they were hugging, not letting go.

"I've got your email address and IM screen name," Cynthia said. "You can't get rid of me now."

"I never heard of such an old lady knowing about all this new-fangled technology," Mrs. VanderHook said as she reached in for a hug herself.

"Oh, Helen," Cynthia said. "You've got to get with the times."

Ben and Lydia grinned.

# 10
# Absolutely Crazy

For the next week, Mrs. VanderHook and Hink kept Ben and Lydia completely preoccupied with their schoolwork and with helping out at the clinic, while the two dads spent nearly every minute in Dr. VanderHook's office going over paperwork or something boring like that. Frank was reviewing the clinic's progress, however he did that. They also had a four-hour church service to go to Sunday morning, which actually was a lot of fun. Everyone was singing and dancing like it was New Year's Eve.

Ben and Lydia, though, were mostly miserable. They desperately wanted to continue the treasure hunt but didn't know what their next step should be. Besides, algebra class with Hink was as much fun as playing tag in the lions' den at the Indianapolis Zoo. Not fun at all.

One thing Lydia did love was taking care of the little kids who came to the clinic with their parents. While the moms and dads were busy in the doctor's office, Lydia and Ben would distract the kids with games like Red Rover or Ring Around the Rosey or anything else they could think up. Her favorite thing was to learn the games the kids themselves had invented, like piling up all the shoes in the middle and having one person trying to straighten them without being hit by the ball the others were throwing at her.

Sometimes the little kids would demand to be held and then would fall asleep in their arms while they tried to keep the other kids entertained. Other times Lydia would pull out a stack of picture books Mrs. VanderHook had brought with her from America and read to the kids while Ben amazed them with card tricks.

Lydia always looked closely at the parents when they came to pick up their kids to see if their faces would reveal what the doctor had said. She felt sick to her stomach when she realized the mother or father had just a short time to live and that this darling little kid she had been playing with would soon become an orphan.

"I can't bear it anymore, Ben," she said one afternoon while they played cards up in Ben's room—a week after Cynthia had left.

"What?" he asked as he laid his last card victoriously. "Being beat all the time?"

Lydia groaned and threw down her cards. "Well, yes, that," she said. "But what I mean is that watching all those mothers and fathers dying of AIDS is just too awful. We have to do something."

"We *are* doing something," he said as he shuffled the cards to begin a new game of Rummy. "We're taking care of their kids while my dad gives them the best medical care possible."

"The best medical care possible *with what he has*," she corrected. "He needs more medicine. He needs more help. He needs more room. Ben, we have to ask our parents for another break from school so we can go find Big Henry."

"You want to go back to Water Street?" Ben asked, picking up all the cards.

"No, not that," she said. "But we have to do something!" She remembered her promise to Cynthia. "Hey, how do you think Cynthia knew what we were up to?"

Ben shrugged and started shuffling the cards.

They were both quiet for a moment.

Just then Frank stuck his head in the door. "Hey, Peachoo," he said, "want to go shopping?"

Lydia laughed. "Yeah, maybe we can catch a movie at the mall, too."

Frank laughed. "No, I'm serious," he said. "I just finished up in the office, and we still have time to do some souvenir shopping before dark. Do you have any money left?"

"A bit," Lydia said. "Come on, Ben. Let's go." She secretly slipped the ring she had been fiddling with into her jeans pocket and followed her dad downstairs.

Lydia sat in the front seat of the Pathfinder and paid attention to where they were going. Ben was sitting in the middle of the backseat so he could see, too. It wasn't too hard to find your way around Monrovia. There were only two main roads going into town, and the downtown area wasn't as big as it had seemed when she'd first arrived.

"Hey, Dad," she said, surprised, "are we going to Water Street?"

"Yeah," he said. "How do you know that?"

Phew. Cynthia hadn't told him.

"Ummm, Ben and I have done a bunch of exploring," she said.

He glanced over at her. "I don't know what to say. You shouldn't come out here by yourself," he said, "but I do admire your sense of adventure."

Lydia smiled, but felt guilty.

Once they arrived at Water Street, Frank couldn't find a parking spot. The traffic was so bad it took almost a half hour to pull down a side street and park just a few blocks away. All three got out of the car and started walking slowly back toward the market area. They must have looked funny—a white man, a white girl, and a Chinese boy—but Lydia didn't care anymore. She scanned the product available in the numerous stalls—from clothes, to cell phone cards, to jewelry, to DVDs, to books.

"Wow!" Ben said. "They have everything here. I should get my mom to come out here."

Frank led them into a stall about the size of a small shed. It was dark and musty inside, but the vendor was friendly. He began describing his products, which were mostly hand-carved musical instruments.

"This one is played like this," he said, picking up a stick on top of a large drum, "to announce the arrival of a boy"—he banged a few beats—"and like this"—he banged out a different rhythm—"to announce the arrival of a girl."

Frank took the sticks from him. "Is this what you do if you end up with a twin boy and girl?" He improvised a mixture of the two beats and got everyone laughing.

The man showed them some more instruments, but Frank spotted a dark little mask hanging in the back corner of the room. "What's that?" he asked.

"Oh, that's just a joke," the man said, "a fun time."

Frank didn't believe him. "Isn't that for ceremonial use?" he said, reaching up for it.

The man stepped in front of him.

"It's nothing," he said. "You would like this rattle much better." It was a dried, hollow gourd surrounded by a net of seashells.

"How common is the secret devil society around here?" Frank asked the man, picking up the rattle and shaking it.

"That's just a story," the man said, walking them toward the door. "Just a story."

Frank shrugged and said, "I know a great Story myself. It's about as bizarre as the one you might tell me, only mine makes you smile at the end." He smiled, and Lydia wondered how anyone could resist his charm. "My Story is about a guy who died on a cross. Can I tell it to you?"

"No stories," the man said, now walking outside into the sunlight. "You just pay me fifteen American dollars for that rattle."

"I'll give you five," Frank said. The man accepted the offer, dropped the rattle in a plastic bag, and sent them on their way.

"You're crazy!" Ben said as soon as they were out of earshot. "You're not supposed to talk about the secret society here."

"I know," Frank said. "But so many people are caught up in secrecy, and there is just no way for them to break free into Truth if someone doesn't start talking. I couldn't resist." He handed Ben the rattle. "Give this to your church," he said.

They walked on in silence for a few minutes. There was so much to look at, but Lydia's mind was on other things. "Dad," she said, "you don't worry about doing risky things as long as you're trying to help people, do you?"

"Well, I have some caution," he said.

"Not really," she said. "You're actually rather crazy—"

He began to interrupt, but she continued.

"Don't worry," she said. "I think that's good. Like on the plane when you just trusted God completely even though we were about to die."

"We weren't about to die."

"Whatever. Anyway, Cynthia said that we don't do risky things and expect God to cover our backs, but we can do risky things if God is covering our backs. Something like that."

"Smart lady," Frank said.

"Yeah," Lydia said. "I think I finally get it."

Frank put his arm around Lydia. "Smart kid," he said.

Lydia looked at Ben, wondering if she should ask her dad to help them find Big Henry. If she should forgive him, basically. Ben caught her eye and nodded, apparently thinking the same thing she was.

Lydia stopped and looked her dad in the eye. "Dad," she said, "we need your help."

Frank leaned up against a wall. "Okay. What's up?" he asked.

"It's about the treasure hunt," Lydia said, glad he was going to listen. "We need help."

"Yeah," Ben said. "We don't want to do anything crazy on our own."

Very smart. Lydia wished she had thought of that one.

"You guys are still doing that?" Frank asked.

"Yeah," Lydia said. "We really want to be able to help Dr. VanderHook's clinic. Ben says he's way too busy."

"He is," Frank said. "What can I do to help you?"

As people milled around them, Lydia told him the story again, starting with the map Ben found under the floorboard in his room. She reminded him about the first clue (*JTEAM—let us ice bed on toll en*) that Ben found at the post office—the one that had been stolen the night they had arrived. Ben told Frank how Lydia had unscrambled the letters and led them to the Temple of Justice.

Frank grinned. "That's my girl!" he said. "Did you find anything there?"

"The next clue," Ben said. "It said *Find Big Henry. Trust God.*"

"Big Henry?" Frank asked. "Who's that?"

Lydia filled him in on what they had learned so far—even confessing that Cynthia had caught them on Water Street before.

"You were looking for a rebel warlord all by yourself?" Frank asked.

Lydia cringed.

Frank waved a hand. "That's in the past," he said. "It sounds like Cynthia taught you a lesson. So, what's our next step?"

"I think we should go into that club over there and ask an adult if they know where we can find Big Henry," she said.

Ben turned sharply. "Are you crazy? A bar here? That's got to be the most dangerous place in the whole city!"

"Maybe because it's Big Henry's hangout," Lydia said.

"Good point," Frank said. "Let's go drop off that rattle in the car while I think about it."

On the way to the car, Lydia stopped to buy some plantain chips—which looked like dried sliced bananas and tasted like potato chips. She felt like part of the crowd. Once she got used to all the commotion, it really was a fun place to be.

"Here's the deal," Frank said once they'd found their car again. "I'll go over to the bar and you guys stay here."

"No way, Dad!" Lydia said, tossing her chips into the front seat of the Pathfinder.

"Way," he said.

"Dad," Lydia said. "You can't leave us out here alone. We'll be safer with you."

"Hmmm . . ." He was clearly thinking this through. "I guess that's true. Besides, this is your treasure hunt." He started walking. "Listen," he said, "you may do this thing, just don't do anything stupid. I'll come as your bodyguard." He walked a few steps farther and then said, "And don't forget to pray."

Lydia prayed as they walked up to the small, cement-block building that looked so much like every other building in the city. Lydia thought she and Ben would get turned away at the door because they were underage, but they walked right up to the bar, and Ben said in his high squeaky voice, "Is Big Henry here?"

It was late afternoon, and not many people were there—maybe only ten or so. Even so, smoke hovered in the room. Some tough-looking black guys were playing pool in the middle of the room and drinking beer. Everyone stopped to look at them. Lydia felt scared to death, but her dad stood there with his feet spread apart and his arms crossed. She had never noticed before how strong he really was. His muscles bulged from under his black T-shirt. He didn't crack a smile.

Then the weirdest thing happened. The bartender looked over his shoulder and yelled, "Boss, a white guy and some kids are here to see you."

They had found Big Henry!

The door was close enough to them that they could have run—and when they saw the tall black man coming toward them with a large gun on his hip, they should have bolted. He was tall, his boulder-sized muscles made her dad's look like pebbles, and his face was scrunched up as if he were angry. The dim light above them reflected off his bald head.

But they didn't run. They smiled as politely as they had when they'd met Lemuel.

"Hello, sir," Ben said.

"What do you want?" the man demanded in the deepest voice Lydia had ever heard. A few other large scary men came up behind him, none of them looking any friendlier than their boss.

"Ummm," Ben said.

*Find Big Henry. And . . .*

"Trust God," Lydia suddenly blurted. She didn't know if she'd said it to Ben, her dad, herself, or Big Henry.

"You missionaries?" he asked with an evil laugh. "Are they sending pawns my way?" He said this last line to his buddies.

Lydia thought of the chess game she had played with Ben the other night and squirmed at the idea of being a pawn up against this fierce opponent. She glanced back at her dad, who had moved closer to them. "We were told to find Big Henry and to trust God," she said.

The men laughed, but Big Henry narrowed his eyes. "Who told you that?" he asked, glancing over at Frank.

"We can't say," Ben said.

"Come 'ere," Big Henry said. He led them into a room behind the bar, where a bunch of wooden chairs were spread in a circle around a rickety card table. Frank was right behind them, but at a word from Big Henry the other men grabbed him. "Hold him until I'm done here," Big Henry said as he closed the door.

Lydia could hear her dad yelling as she was shoved into a chair.

# 11
# You'd Better Believe It

**W**hat do you want?" Big Henry demanded, looking back and forth between them.

"The next clue," Ben said quietly. "Then we'll leave you alone." Ben was sitting in the chair next to her.

"Who sent you?"

"The previous clue," Ben said.

All Lydia could think about was her dad.

"You're just kids!" Big Henry hit the wall with his fist.

Neither one of them said anything.

"I was waiting for you to come before you were even born." Big Henry's voice was shaking.

"What do you mean?" Lydia asked. She wished she were feeling as calm as Ben looked.

"It doesn't matter," Big Henry said, suddenly getting himself under control. "I'm going to do this anyway."

"Do what?" Lydia asked. *Dad!*

The man pulled out a gun and turned to Ben. "You!" he said. "Do you buy into this whole Christian rubbish like your sister does?"

"She's not my sister."

"Answer the question."

"Of course I do," Ben said quietly. "That's why I'm here."

The man cursed under his breath. He turned to Lydia. "What about you?"

Lydia's mind flitted back to the diamond she found on the beach and how that had been such a clear indication to her that God was in control. "Yes," she said. "I do."

"Wrong answer," Big Henry growled. "Now I have to kill you." He lifted the gun and pointed it at Ben's head.

"Wait!" Lydia called. She looked around frantically. Why wasn't her dad breaking in here to save them? "You have to kill us because we trust God?" Her voice was shaking.

"Those are my orders," the rebel said.

"So if we said we didn't trust God, then what?"

Big Henry looked confused for a minute. "You don't trust God?"

"We do," Lydia said, even though she thought she *really* must be crazy for admitting it, "but I don't get why you need to kill us for that. What difference does it make to you?"

"All the difference. And I'll give you one more chance to change your mind. Stand up if you want to renounce your silly faith." He raised his gun again. "I'll count to three, and if you're not standing up by then, you'll be dead. One."

Lydia looked at Ben. He looked scared. But he didn't stand up. "Two."

Lydia sat back in her chair. *Trust God. Trust God. Trust God.* "Three."

Big Henry didn't shoot. Instead, he punched the wall again. Ben and Lydia stared at him.

"How did you know I wasn't going to kill you?" the man said.

"You're not?" Ben said the words in a whisper, and then fainted.

Lydia jumped up and ran to Ben's chair to pull him back up. "If you're not going to kill us, why did you do this to us in the first place?" she demanded angrily. "That was a very bad joke."

"Are you calling my honor a joke?" he asked angrily.

"What are you talking about?" Lydia asked, more concerned about Ben than anything else—and glad to see that he was reviving.

"For ten years I have been waiting for this day I could be free of my obligation," Big Henry said. Which made Lydia mad because he must have thought they were younger than ten. "And the second you walk out of this place, I *will* be free," he continued.

"What are you talking about?" she asked.

Just then Frank burst into the room. A man rushed in after him, but Big Henry waved his gun. "Let him in," he said. "Sit down," he said in a harsh voice to Frank. "Get out," he said to the other man.

"What's going on?" Frank demanded.

"It's okay, Dad," Lydia said. She had enough adrenaline pumping to run to America and back, but she somehow managed to walk calmly back to her chair and sit down. She turned back to Big Henry. "What are you talking about?"

Big Henry sighed and pulled a chair in front of himself to straddle. He sat down noisily.

Frank sat down too, looking very worried.

"I was just doing my job," Big Henry began. "Ten years ago. Back then I was trying to rid this city of those awful UN workers, and just as I was ready to blow the head off this one scrawny white dude, he turned on me. Apparently he had a needle in his hand with some powerful drug that knocked me out. When I came to, he was still there. He made some speech about how he spared my life and the life of my family—my small brother was there—and for some weird reason it affected me. I felt like God was—" he cut himself short. "Forget it," he said.

Lydia thought of Cynthia's prayer on the beach and smiled. It *was* weird when the Holy Spirit convicted you of something.

"Here's what you need to know," Big Henry continued. "The scrawny dude told me that someday someone would show up here saying the kind of junk you just said—and that I was to threaten your life if you called yourselves Christians."

"He must have been the guy who planned the treasure hunt!" Ben said to Lydia. He was sweating and his voice quavered.

"Shut up and listen," Big Henry said. "If you were not true Christians, then all I had to do was let you go."

"But we are true Christians—" Lydia began, quickly letting her voice fade when he glared at her.

"But since you do take all this junk seriously," he continued, staring her down, "then I have two obligations."

Lydia and Ben squirmed in their seats, looking at him anxiously, but saying nothing.

"I'm only doing this because I promised," Big Henry said, even looking a bit nervous. "My honor is on the line."

No one said anything. Lydia wanted to ask what 'honor' was, but figured now was not a good time for questions. It must have something to with his pride.

"First, I have to ask you why you believe."

Ben and Lydia looked at each other. Here they were missionaries and they didn't know what to say. Lydia looked at her dad, and he immediately started giving his testimony.

"I asked *them*," the rebel said, cutting him off.

Lydia suddenly knew what her testimony would be. She took a deep breath. "I don't think I really believed 'this junk' until just last week," she said.

"What?" the man asked.

Lydia told him the story of Arway and Promise and of the little kids at the clinic—and even of the diamond ring she'd found on the beach. She hadn't told Ben or her dad, but she suddenly felt glad to share the experience with this dangerous man so different from herself. As she talked, no one moved and everyone watched her face intently.

"I had been feeling sorry for myself all my life that my mom died when I was young, but it turns out that God loves me way more than she could have," she said softly. "God really does care what's happening in the world—and to me! And by giving me that little heart-shaped diamond, I knew He was also in control. He can do anything."

The ring was actually in her pocket right now, but she didn't say anything about that.

Big Henry cleared his throat. It was weird to see such a hardened man close to tears. Frank reached over and touched his daughter's hand, and she smiled at him.

"Okay," Big Henry said. "My other obligation is that I have to tell you to look more closely at the postcard you have. At the top right-hand corner."

Lydia looked at Ben. He shrugged, clearly confused.

Big Henry stood up. "Now get out of here," he said. "And don't show your face here again. I won't be so nice next time."

Ben and Lydia quickly got up and ran to the door. Frank strode just as quickly behind them.

Just before they stepped out of the room, Lydia turned around. "Thank you, sir." She ran back and gave him a hug. Just for a second. And then they got out of the dirty, smoky building and ran as fast as they could. They kept running, even Lydia's dad, until they reached the car. They just wanted to get home.

"What happened in there?" Frank asked as he cut into traffic to get onto the busy street. "I can't believe I was so stupid! I never should have let you talk me into this!"

"I know!" Lydia yelled. "It was crazy! But we're alive!" She couldn't believe it. She felt the same way she had after the minivan she was in last year spun out on the freeway and got broadsided by an oncoming pickup truck. None of the passengers suffered anything more than bruises from the seatbelt.

"We're alive!" Ben echoed. "And we got the next clue!"

Lydia was sitting in the front seat again, and Ben shook her bucket seat from the back as he roared out a shout of victory. Clearly, everyone's adrenaline was going.

Even Frank got into the excitement of the moment. He laughed and yelled, "Man alive! That sure was wild!" He quickly caught himself, though. "But don't you ever, ever, *ever* ask me to do anything like that again."

"What postcard do you think he was talking about?" Lydia asked Ben.

"I don't know," Ben said.

"Was there a postcard in the pile of mail you got from that post office?" Frank asked.

Ben's eyes lit up. "Yes, there was!" he said. "I know exactly where it is."

As soon as they got home, Ben and Lydia ran up to Ben's room to look at the postcard.

"Where is it?" Lydia asked, rummaging through his desk.

"It's right here," he said, pulling it from the mirror. "It was in the pile of mail I got from the post office when I got the first clue. I liked it, so I stuck it there."

It was a hand-drawn, black-and-white picture of Monrovia. Ben pulled it up close to his face to get a better look. Lydia put her head right up beside his. All she could see was one of the background buildings.

"I don't get it," Ben said, handing the postcard to her.

"The letters on this building look like 'JFK,'" Lydia said, staring closely at the top right-hand corner.

"That's the hospital. Maybe we should take the stamp off to see if anything is written under there."

Lydia flipped the postcard over and tried to pick at the stamp. It wouldn't come off that way, so they went downstairs to heat up some water to try to steam it off.

The adults were sitting in the living room, obviously talking about the encounter with Big Henry. Mrs. VanderHook rushed over and kissed Ben. "Oh, honey," she said, "that must have been terrifying." She gushed over her boy, and Hink drilled both kids with questions about the experience until Ben finally got the stamp wet enough to peel off. There were some tiny letters under it, and the kids were about to run upstairs to check it out with a magnifying glass, but Mrs. VanderHook made them stay to eat leftover dinner first. She kept asking Ben if he was okay.

"Check it out," Ben said once they were back upstairs. They looked at it with the magnifying glass together:

**One would get this from the LMB. It is your decoder.**
**OJ _SG MS_B MOEBHOR, IS VS SMUBWV ON**
**WRWCRVS_N LSH VCB LONRM PMGB.**

"Get what?" Ben asked.

"And what's the LMB?" Lydia continued.

They began to list as many ideas as they could think of: Licensed Motor Boats, Leftwing Mayor Box, Library Middle Branch, Land Management Bureau, Little Munchkin Boy. Lydia came up with that last one.

"Hey, Lydia," Ben said cautiously. "I really liked what you said to Big Henry."

Lydia blushed.

"I can't believe you didn't tell me about the diamond, though," he said.

If she had been blushing before, she probably looked like a beet dipped in ketchup now.

"Sorry," she said.

"You don't need to apologize," he said. "It's just that you're usually so . . ."

"Talkative?" she said.

"Yeah, I guess," he said. "I just thought you would have told me."

Lydia shrugged.

"So what are you going to do with the diamond?" he asked. "It must be worth thousands of dollars."

"Thousands?" Lydia didn't realize it would be that much. Still, she didn't need to think about her answer. "I'm going to keep it," she said. "It means a lot to me."

The next morning, Ben and Lydia brainstormed about what LMB could mean as they played with the kids waiting at the clinic. "Arway!" Lydia suddenly exclaimed when she noticed the woman walking past the children toward the clinic door.

"Ah! Lydia," the young woman replied. She smiled kindly, revealing her natural beauty, but her face looked sad. "My heart is warm to see you."

"I'm so glad to see you, too!" Lydia said, running to Arway's side. "I've been thinking of you constantly. We haven't given up on looking for Promise, you know."

Arway reached up and patted Lydia's head. "It's okay."

Lydia hadn't noticed before, but Arway wasn't much taller than Lydia, and she seemed so much frailer this time. "What are you doing here?" Lydia suddenly asked.

"I'm here to see the doctor," Arway said. Her voice broke, and Lydia looked at her closely.

"Oh, Arway!" Lydia said, nearly crying. Because she knew. They both knew. Arway was dying.

# 12
# Dark Shadows

**B**ut, Lydia," Ben pleaded, "we're so close!"

"I don't care," Lydia whispered, trying to get past him in the staircase. He was blocking her way. "I don't care about a stupid treasure hunt. I don't care if we never see another diamond. Just let me go."

"Lydia, maybe the money can help us take care of Arway," Ben whispered.

"Nothing will help Arway anymore, stupid," Lydia whispered. She felt bad for calling him a name, but she didn't know what else to do with her anger. Arway was sleeping on her dad's couch at the bottom of the stairs. Her dad had moved his stuff over to the clinic. Lydia had convinced her dad and the VanderHooks to let the dying woman stay with them during her last days.

"Lydia," Ben said, "I need your help."

"Ben," Lydia said, exasperated, "just let me go."

He did. And Lydia didn't feel any better for it. She slunk past him and sat on the floor of the living room with her back against Arway's couch, trying to concentrate on her algebra homework. Just as she was starting to forget about her frustration, she heard Arway's voice.

"I'm scared," Arway whispered.

Lydia turned around and saw Arway lying on her side, staring into space. Lydia gently rubbed her back. What else could she do?

"I knew de end would come. I just didn't know it come so soon," Arway whispered.

"When did you first know you had AIDS?" Lydia asked.

She told Lydia that they had seen signs of it in Arway's husband first. He died a year before Promise disappeared. Arway had come to this clinic with him many times. His sister had died, leaving behind a two-year-old child, and the religious tradition was to take the blood of the orphaned child and to pass it among the family to fend off whatever stole the life of the mother. They took a razor blade and cut the baby's shoulder. That blade was then passed around the circle for each person to use on himself or herself.

Lydia was horrified.

"Didn't you know about AIDS?" Lydia asked.

Arway hadn't. She had never heard of the disease and certainly didn't know how it was passed around. She and her husband, John, lived far from town then and hadn't been educated yet. She didn't know the Lord then, either, or that His power was stronger than their traditions. She didn't even know why her sister-in-law had died.

"I knew so little," Arway said sadly. "If only we knew . . ."

Lydia murmured her sympathy.

Arway kept talking. The worst thing for her was that her husband hadn't walked with God. She herself hadn't known the Lord until after he died. Now she was afraid that she wouldn't see him in heaven. "And I shore do love dat man," she said.

Lydia continued to rub her new friend's back as Arway shook. When she became still again and lifted her head to stare into the dark shadows in the corner of the room, Lydia asked, "How did you come to know the Lord?"

This made Arway smile through her tears. They had moved to town when John got sick. John needed medical attention, and they were coming to the clinic almost every day. Dr. VanderHook, of course, talked of God constantly, but Arway was too caught up in caring for John to listen. But one day when she was walking home from John's grave, she started praying. Just like Dr. VanderHook said they could. "And God was dere," Arway said.

Lydia smiled. She was glad that she could relate. She used to think she was a Christian just because her dad was, but now, ever since her day on the beach, she believed God for herself—and it made all the difference.

Arway didn't know how to read, but she wanted to hear more about God, so she went to a church and listened to the Bible being read. John didn't come back to life and Promise didn't come home, but she knew she was going to be all right. "Now Jesus be my best Friend and dat little church be my family."

"You don't need to be afraid, Arway," Lydia said after a moment.

The conversation turned to other topics and the two talked late into the night.

The next morning, Lydia knew exactly what she had to do. "Dad," she said, waking him up and staring into his still sleepy eyes.

"Good morning, Lydia," her dad said. "It's Sunday. Why are you up so early?"

"Dad," Lydia said again, "we have to find Promise."

Her dad sighed. "We're doing everything we can. It's not for lack of effort that that young girl is not showing up."

It was true. Frank had contacted some NGOs who worked with displaced children. And before she'd left, Cynthia had looked through hundreds of pictures on her Web photo album, pictures taken all over West Africa, looking for a girl with a birthmark between her eyes. She'd found nothing.

"Why don't we just call all the orphanages in Africa and describe Promise to them? She has that birthmark, remember?"

"We've tried that some," Frank said. "But there are too many orphanages and too few workers there. People don't have time to answer our questions. Besides," he continued, "most orphans don't live in orphanages. Nearly half of the families in most African countries have at least one orphan living in their homes."

"We could hire one of those artists that cops use," Lydia said, "—you know, the guys who can draw a picture of someone just by hearing a description."

"And what would we do with the picture?"

"I don't know. Blow it up to billboard size and drive around Africa with it."

Frank laughed but put a hand on Lydia's shoulder lovingly. "I'm not laughing at you, Lydia," he said. "I am laughing at how similar you are to your mother. You won't give up, will you?"

"No, I won't!" Lydia said.

Her dad sighed. "We just don't have that kind of money, Peachoo."

"I thought you'd say that," Lydia replied. "And that's why I want to give you this." She opened her hand and let the diamond ring sit on her palm right in front of her dad's eyes.

Lydia got the reaction she was hoping for. He stared at it for a moment, as if not daring to touch it, but his eyes said it all. "So this is it, huh?" He had been in the room when she told Big Henry the story, but he hadn't asked her about it later. She could see now how curious he must have been. She was glad he had waited.

She nodded.

"Lydia, you can't give that up," he said.

"How much do you think it's worth?"

Frank picked the ring up and looked more closely at the diamond. "It's huge and it looks flawless—I would guess at least ten thousand dollars," he answered. He held it out to her. "But I know how important this ring is to you."

"Finding Promise is worth it," Lydia said, pressing it back into his hand.

"What if it doesn't work?" Frank asked. "What if we spend all this time and money looking for Promise and we don't find her?"

"We will."

"I like your positive thinking," he said, "but I also want to know that you're prepared for the worst. I don't want to see your hopes get dashed."

"What difference does it make? My hopes are high now, and if I try not to hope so much it'll hurt just as much now as it would later."

"Good point," her dad said. "Fine. I'll talk about it with the others."

That was good enough for Lydia. She left her dad and went to wake up Ben. "Ben," she said, "let me see that postcard."

"Huh?"

"The postcard!"

"It's the middle of the night," he grumbled.

"No, it's not," she said. "It's like seven thirty in the morning."

He groaned and pulled a pillow over his head. "Go away."

"No!" Lydia persisted. "We'll be going to church in an hour or so and then I'll have to take care of Arway after that. You wanted my help, and I'm ready to help. So wake up." With that she yanked the pillow from his hands and hit him with it.

Ben sat up quickly and grabbed the pillow from her. "Give that to me," he said. He pulled the pillowcase off and unzipped the inside cover. He reached into the feathers and pulled out the postcard.

Lydia laughed. "Good hiding spot."

"Good to have you back," he said.

By eight fifteen no one had called them down for breakfast, and Lydia started to wonder what was going on. "Shhh!" she said.

Loud voices drifted up the stairs.

"What's going on?" Ben asked.

They slunk down the steps and discovered the voices were coming from the kitchen. Arway was somehow still sleeping through all the commotion.

Lydia heard her teacher's voice first. "I don't agree with Frank," Hink was saying. "She found it while staying here under the VanderHooks' roof, and the money should go to them."

"She didn't find it under their roof, though," Frank said. "And she gave it up for a specific reason."

"Perhaps she doesn't realize that we will be helping many more people by improving the clinic," Dr. VanderHook said, "than by seeking out one lost girl."

"Peter!" Mrs. VanderHook said. "Don't be selfish!"

"I'm hardly being selfish!" he said in a voice Lydia had never heard him use. Lydia was standing by the door now and could see his face turning red. "I don't want a cent of that money for myself!"

"Are you trying to say that I want it for myself?" Frank asked angrily.

"No, Frank," Mrs. VanderHook said.

"The diamond belongs to my daughter," Frank said as little beads of sweat formed on his forehead, "and no one can argue whether her heart is in the right place. You see how she cares about that woman. And she didn't ask to reserve any for herself—"

"No one is arguing with that, Frank," Mrs. VanderHook cut in. "Peter is just trying to say that she might not know what would be the most effective."

"That's true," Hink said, smiling a little. "She's being more like Mary Magdalene—dumping all her fine perfume on the one she loves."

Everyone was quiet . . . just as Lydia cleared her throat. They all turned to see her standing in the doorway with Ben just behind her.

"You should be more quiet," Lydia said, blushing. "Arway is sleeping."

"Umm, Lydia," Ben said, "I don't think she's sleeping." He sank down into a chair and put his head in his hands.

Lydia turned around. Arway was lying on the couch just as she had been, but suddenly everything looked wrong. Lydia pushed Ben aside and ran to Arway's side. She placed her hands on the woman's back just as she had done last night, but her friend's body held no warmth.

"Daddy!" she called—but he was right behind her. So was Dr. VanderHook.

"Oh, honey," her dad said, taking Lydia into his arms and pulling her away. "Oh, baby."

Lydia pushed her face into her dad's shoulder as Dr. VanderHook felt for a pulse.

"I'm sorry," the doctor said. "She's gone."

Mrs. VanderHook began to wail. Surprised by the outburst, Lydia forgot her own misery for a moment to look at her, but Frank whispered in her ear, "Go ahead and cry, Peachoo. This is how Africans mourn the loss of those they love."

Lydia didn't need any convincing. Her sorrow piled up inside and around her so that she couldn't hold in her tears any longer. She leaned into her dad again and let all her emotion out—making noises she hadn't made since she was a little kid. But she wasn't embarrassed. She felt connected to everyone in the room, and comforted by their strong emotion. Mrs. VanderHook was down on her knees, Ben had joined in the loud wailing, and the men were all crying, too. Even Hink seemed to have overcome any embarrassment and was crying herself.

A half hour passed. Finally the doctor got up and went outside. His face was streaked with tears. The neighbors, who had been outside the clinic and had loudly joined in the wailing themselves, reached over to touch him.

Lydia was exhausted.

"We'll do more mourning soon enough," Mrs. VanderHook said softly when the crying had subsided. "Ben, go find someone to run the news to Arway's church. They should be meeting right now."

"Yes, ma'am." Ben went outside and passed on the message, and then sat down on the steps with his dad.

"Helen," Hink said to Ben's mom, "let's prepare the body."

Mrs. VanderHook nodded and stood up.

Frank led Lydia to the other couch. She didn't have any more tears for now, but she was glad to curl up in her dad's comforting arms—way too big for his lap now, but managing to pull it off anyway—as she watched the women wash and wrap Arway with love and respect. Frank began to hum, and Lydia fell asleep.

Lydia woke up and saw that Arway was gone. That beautiful young mother would never see her little girl again.

The space in Lydia's heart was just as empty as that couch.

"Peachoo?" Frank stuck his head into the room. "You awake?"

She nodded.

"Come get something to eat."

She stood up and walked to the kitchen.

"Honey, I'm sorry you had to hear that conversation in the kitchen."

Lydia shrugged.

"We'll find Promise," her dad said as he set a piece of toast and a boiled egg in front of her.

"It doesn't matter, Dad," Lydia said as she peeled the egg. "I think Dr. VanderHook is right. The money should go to the clinic. We'll never find Promise anyway. And even if we did, what's the point now?"

Ben and Mrs. VanderHook came into the room just as Ben was emphatically saying, "But why?"

"We don't know that, honey," his mother said, looking very concerned.

Ben sat down across from Lydia. His eyes were red.

"Dad should have been able to heal her," he said, completely ignoring Frank and Lydia. "What's the point of being a doctor if you can't even heal people?"

No one said anything, and a moment later Dr. VanderHook ran into the room.

"Honey!" Mrs. VanderHook said. "What's wrong?"

"That fellow Big Henry is here," the doctor said, looking nervous.

The two kids looked at each other. "What does he want?" Ben asked.

"He's here to talk to Lydia."

"What!" Frank stood up and went to the door. Everyone followed.

# 13

# Off the Beaten Path

Big Henry looked out of place among all the people loitering by the clinic doors. His muscular arms were the size of most patients' legs, and his black motorcycle was twice as big as the neighbors' dirt bikes. Lydia couldn't tell if he felt out of place, though. His mirrored sunglasses covered his eyes, and he stood leaning casually against the house. He didn't move even while everyone filed toward him.

Frank stuck out his hand. "How are you, sir?" he said.

Big Henry ignored the hand, grunted, and shifted the dirty toothpick from one side of his mouth to the other. He looked at Lydia. "I think I know where you might find that girl," he said.

Lydia forgot all about being scared. "What! Where? How—"

Big Henry cracked a smile. "She's in Sierra Leone. One of my people just confirmed it this morning."

Lydia ran to hug him. "Thank you, thank you, thank you!"

Big Henry quickly brushed her off. "I can't be one hundred percent sure that it's her, but she does have that birthmark you mentioned."

"But how did you—"

"Let's not worry about the how, okay? Now, what do you want to do about it?"

Lydia turned to her dad and practically fell in front of him. "Let's go get her!" The emotions inside of her seemed too crazy and abundant to contain. "Please, Daddy!"

"Where is she staying?" Frank asked, unmoved. "An orphanage?"

"Naw," Big Henry responded, resuming his old pose against the side of the building. "She's with a family."

"She may not want to leave," Frank said to Lydia. "But I think we should go there to meet her."

Lydia kissed her dad's hands, grabbed Ben and hugged him, and then turned back to Big Henry.

"Uh-uh!" he said, when she moved in for another hug. "Leave me out of this. I'll just give you the information and you can do your business." He pulled out a piece of paper and handed it to Frank. "Find this village, and you'll find the girl," he said.

"Do we owe you anything?" Dr. VanderHook asked when Big Henry turned to walk away.

Big Henry's eyes flickered for a moment, but then he shrugged. "Naw," he said. "Just returning a good deed." He lifted his sunglasses and winked at Lydia, and then, without another word, straddled the motorcycle and left with a loud roar. Lydia watched until his cloud of dust disappeared.

"What good deed is he talking about?" Lydia asked Ben.

Ben shrugged. "Maybe we helped him to believe in God."

Lydia's face lit up. "Really?"

"Great news here," the doctor said, "but I've got to go sit down. I'm beat."

"I think we've caused him more interruptions than help," Dad said as the doctor walked away.

"Don't think that for a second," Mrs. VanderHook said. "You folks have brought new energy to this place."

"I agree with Frank," Hink said. "I hope you kids have at least dropped that crazy treasure hunt idea."

Lydia just shrugged.

"I think we're going to have to take a little break from algebra tomorrow, Mrs. Hinkle," Frank said. "These kids have got another lesson coming their way."

Ben stared at Frank, ignoring the tutor's harrumph. "Does that mean I get to go, too?"

Frank looked at Mrs. VanderHook with a smile.

She nodded reluctantly.

"Of course it does!" Frank said. He grabbed Lydia's hand and put his other hand around Ben's shoulders, leading them back to the house. "Let's work on getting us some visas to Sierra Leone."

They say that if you got one thing done in Monrovia, it's been a good day. Lydia's dad got two things done. Monday morning he took the kids straight to the US embassy and used his charm to convince the woman in charge that all three of them needed to go on this trip. And then, with the temporary visas in hand, he headed to the UN building to book three plane tickets to Kabala—to return two days before he and Lydia and Mrs. Hinkle were to leave Africa.

"I didn't know we could fly free with the UN," Ben said.

"You're an NGO worker," Frank said. "That gives you certain privileges."

The five days of waiting for their trip to Sierra Leone passed quickly. They had to endure a heartbreaking funeral for Arway—though Lydia was amazed to see the hope and joy of the people who had loved Arway even more than she had. Ben and Lydia also had to go back to their studies every morning with the wicked witch of the west—who seemed even more intent on working their brains out now that they had a "little vacation" coming up. Plus they needed to decipher the last clue. Both of them felt the deadline for Lydia's departure looming over them.

"I know you're not crazy about flying, Peachoo," her dad joked the night before they were to leave for Sierra Leone. "Why don't you just stay here, and Ben and I will go meet Promise?"

"Very funny, Dad!" she said.

Ben laughed, though.

"Besides," Frank continued, "you have so much trouble waking up in the morning on school days, I'm sure tomorrow you would prefer to just sleep in on your day off. You always beg me to let you sleep on Saturdays . . ."

"Dad!" she said over Ben's laughter. "That's a dumb joke."

Lydia almost did sleep in, though. She couldn't fall asleep the night before, and when she finally did, she dreamed that Big Henry stood laughing at them from the doorway of the house where Promise lived—and she woke with a start.

"Dear God," she whispered into the darkness, "please let us find Promise. I know You've got things under control. I know Arway is safe with You. Please let Promise be safe, too." She fell back asleep and didn't wake up until her dad shook her.

"I hope you have your things packed, Peachoo," he said. "We're leaving in five minutes."

In the old days, back in the United States, the announcement of five minutes would have sent Lydia screaming more than would a sighting of Orlando Bloom. As it was, she kept her head on the pillow for another minute or so before grabbing the first pair of jeans and T-shirt her hands touched. She wolfed down a bowl of oatmeal and then washed her hands and face with cold water in the kitchen sink. She rebraided her unwashed hair in the car.

By the time they got checked in at the airport, Lydia was fully alert. "I can't wait!" she kept saying.

"Remember, it might not be the right girl," Frank reminded her.

"Oh ye of little faith," Ben said.

Frank grinned.

Frank had arranged ahead of time to rent a tricked-out Jeep and had carefully mapped out the way to the place where Promise might be living. It was supposed to be easy. But after they left the airport, it took about ten thousand hours to find the place where they were getting the Jeep. Then it was out of gas, and they had to take another ten thousand hours to find a gas station that actually had gas. Plus Frank insisted that they head to the market to get several baskets of food—way more than they would use in three days. Frank was geeked, though—all excited to be using his GPS receiver and all the other gadgets he had borrowed from Dr. VanderHook for backcountry driving.

"You're like a little kid, Dad," Lydia said, feeling rather grumpy.

"It's cool!" her dad said, proving her point. "Did you know that we're going to find our way to a remote village in Africa using some of the most advanced technology developed in the world? The Global Positioning System is the only fully functional satellite navigation system in use today. More than two dozen GPS satellites orbit the earth, transmitting radio signals that allow GPS receivers to determine their location, speed, and direction."

"Cool!" Ben said, leaning in close to look at the receiver. "Let me see!"

"Don't encourage him," Lydia said.

"What are you talking about, Lyd?" Frank said. "He's a part of the brotherhood. Brothers like gadgets."

"That's something you just won't understand, *Lyd*," Ben said, grinning.

The "brothers" went back to checking out the tricks the stupid little machine could do while Lydia rolled her eyes. "Can't we just get going?" she said.

"Oh, yeah," Frank said. "Let's go."

Lydia soon regretted urging him to hurry. Even though they drove slowly over the rough road, her stomach felt queasy within a half hour.

"This is better than off-roading in Colorado!" her dad said happily as he climbed a hill on a path surrounded by monster-sized houseplants. "And we get to go way north, almost to the border of Guinea."

Lydia groaned.

They crossed over streams using rickety palm log bridges and drove through potholes that swallowed the car. They squashed a line of driver ants that her dad said could take down a large animal and eat its flesh. They climbed up dirt cliffs as the sand fell out beneath them and roared down slopes at terrifying speeds. Ben sat in the front and whooped him on, while Lydia sat in the back holding her stomach.

"You're going to kill us, Dad!" she hollered every once in awhile. It was like talking to a fish in an aquarium. He didn't pay a bit of attention.

By the time evening started to fall, they hadn't reached their destination yet. Frank pulled over to study the map. "We might just have to sleep out here in the Jeep tonight," he said happily. "I don't want to get lost in the dark — and we still have about an hour to go."

"Dad!" Lydia protested. "Don't the lions come out at night?"

"Not much big game out here, Peachoo," Frank said. "We'll probably get a beautiful view of some antelope, though. And maybe some pigs."

"Oh, look!" Ben said. "There are so many birds!" He pointed up into the trees where birds with bright iridescent amethyst backs and pure white bellies circled.

"They've been there all along," Lydia said. "You just didn't see them because you were so busy looking for rocks to jump." She swatted a mosquito that had managed to come in, even though the windows were tightly closed. She wasn't sure if it was the kind of mosquito that spreads malaria, but she was glad she had been taking her antimalaria medicine faithfully every day.

"And perhaps some tiger cats and chimps," Frank said quietly.

Lydia heard him loud and clear, though. "Dad! We have to find that hotel!"

"All right," Frank said. "It might not be as far as I think."

It wasn't. They arrived at the next town within fifteen minutes and found the hotel right away. It would have been rated negative five stars in the States in terms of comfort and cleanliness, but Lydia was glad for the safety it offered.

"Tomorrow," she said when her dad wrapped mosquito netting around her.

"Yes, tomorrow," he said. He kissed her on the forehead and whispered, "Have I ever told you how much I love you?"

Lydia grinned. "Only a million times."

"Good."

Lydia fell asleep hoping and praying that someone loved Promise as much as her dad loved her.

Lydia opened her eyes. She sat up and saw her dad studying a map. Ben was playing with the GPS receiver. She couldn't believe they had woken before her. She pulled off the mosquito netting.

"So, do you know the way?" she asked her dad, trying to pretend she'd been awake for ages.

"Yeah," her dad answered without looking up. "I think I've got it figured out. But we certainly are going into the middle of nowhere."

"I thought that's where we were," Ben said.

Frank laughed. "Just wait! You'll understand where 'nowhere' is pretty soon."

They packed up their few things and checked out of the hotel.

As they drove away from the town, Ben and Lydia caught on to what Frank was talking about. In the city of Monrovia, they were in a constant crowd of people, night and day. During their back-road journey so far they had seen people walking alongside the road on a regular basis. But now there wasn't even a road to walk along.

"Your dad would go nuts out here, Ben," Frank said. "He hardly has what he needs to run the clinic as it is—and he's right in the middle of the city with pharmacies every mile."

"If there are so many pharmacies," Lydia asked, "why does Dr. VanderHook keep saying he needs more medicine?"

"The kind they sell at the pharmacies is not the kind he needs. Also, much of the stuff sold in the marketplace is expired."

"Do you think there are any doctors out here?" Ben asked.

"I doubt it," Frank said. "Maybe they have locals providing care to the sick, but I doubt there's anyone here with a medical license."

"Does your dad have a medical license?" Lydia asked Ben.

Ben shrugged.

"Of course he does, Lyd," her dad said. "He couldn't operate a clinic without one. When he first came to Monrovia he had to have his US license sent over here, and then he had to appear before the Liberian Medical Board. That's a process that—"

"The what?" Lydia asked, sitting up.

"The Liberian Medical Board," her dad said, looking confused. "What's the problem?"

"He got his license from the *Liberian Medical Board*, Ben," Lydia said, practically bumping her head on the top of the Jeep as she jumped in excitement.

Ben's eyes slowly lit up. "Yee-ahhh," he said. "LMB!"

"Am I missing something?" Frank asked.

"No, but we were!" Lydia responded. "We have to look at the license, Ben! I bet we'll find it!"

Ben nodded thoughtfully and Frank exploded. "Find *what*?"

"Dad," Lydia said, grabbing his arm, "the treasure hunt! Remember?"

"Oh, yeah. The one that nearly got us killed at the hands of a rebel leader."

Just at that second the Jeep nearly dipped into a giant pothole, and Frank jerked the wheel quickly to the right. "Woo-hoo!" he called as the vehicle spun around in the middle of the dirt road. "That's what I'm talking about!" He hit the gas and tore around the numerous potholes littering the road for the next several miles. "Did you see that, Ben?" he hollered. "That's some awesome off-road driving—on the road!"

Ben laughed.

"And, look, Lyd!" her dad said. "There's the village."

"Dad, you've got ADHD," Lydia said with a laugh.

Frank grinned. "Proud of it," he said. He slowed the vehicle down to a respectable speed and crawled into town. Little kids ran up to them, coming out of nowhere, and surrounded the car. They were laughing and talking with great excitement in some language Lydia could not understand. She studied the girls—looking for one about the age of eight who had a birthmark between her eyes.

By the time Frank pulled the car to a stop in the center of the village, a crowd of people surrounded them—men, women, and children.

"Hello," Frank said, smiling.

"Ello! Ello! Ello!" the children called, laughing.

An old woman stepped out of the crowd and bowed deeply to Frank and to Ben and then took Lydia's hands and kissed them. "Welcome," she said.

"You speak English!" Frank said.

"Yes, I lived in Freetown for many years," she said, turning back to Frank. "But the others speak Limba. How can we help you?"

Dad bowed deeply himself. "You are gracious, old woman," he said. Lydia stared at him for a moment, thinking he had insulted her, but quickly saw that his words pleased the lady. "We would be glad to share a meal with you and to offer you some news."

"More news?" the lady said. "Our village has become a busy place lately. But we will talk of that later. Where do you visit from?"

"We are Americans, but we have been living and working in Liberia," Frank began.

The woman addressed her people in their language, apparently translating Frank's words. The people nodded and smiled.

Frank continued. "We serve the Christian God and are saved by his Son, Jesus."

The woman translated—and Lydia squirmed. This was not supposed to be a missionary trip. Her dad was going to get them all mad before they would have a chance to find Promise.

But her dad went on. "My name is Frank Barnes, and this is my daughter, Lydia"—Lydia smiled—"and our friend Ben VanderHook." Ben waved. "Ben's father runs a medical clinic in Monrovia. Their family has been living there for almost four years."

He placed a hand on Lydia's arm while the woman translated. Lydia got the message: *Shut up and quit worrying*. He knew what he was doing. Lydia sighed deeply and settled down. She had waited this long; she figured she could wait a bit longer.

# 14
# The Gift That Came Back

Y ou are very welcome here," the woman said. "We are just ready to begin the worship service of our Lord Jesus Christ. After that we shall eat. We do not have much to share, but what we have, we give gladly. Will you join us?"

Frank offered up that contagious grin. "How exciting!" he said. "We'd love to join you in worship. As for the meal, we have brought plenty. We would be honored if you would receive it." He pulled from the back of the Jeep a bushel basket filled with potatoes and onions and oranges and bread. "Please accept our gift."

The old woman bowed again, smiling. She nodded to a young man and spoke a few words in her own language.

He stepped forward, eyes wide, and took the basket from Frank. *"Walli ne!"* the young man said. *"Walli ne!"*

While the meal was being prepared, the old woman took the foreigners to the center of the village under a canopy made from banana tree branches. It was surprisingly cool in that shade. The villagers formed a wide circle. Frank, with Ben and Lydia following suit, sat cross-legged on the ground.

The worship service was shorter than the one in Monrovia, only about two hours. They spent the first hour singing, and Lydia found herself worshipping God more than she ever had before, even though she was just humming along. She couldn't understand the words, but she could certainly understand their love for Christ. The second hour was spent mostly praying. Some people would stand up to speak for five or ten minutes at a time, and then they would go back to praying. Lydia lost some interest in this part of the service, and couldn't help looking around for a little girl with a birthmark on her forehead.

When the service was over, the old woman invited the guests to remain where they were. No one else left either. "Please tell us where you came from," the old woman said, settling in for a long conversation.

The conversation turned out to be lovely. The old woman had a wonderful sense of humor and often laughed warmly as Frank talked—which, of course, only got him cutting more jokes. Lydia and Ben were asked questions now and then—about how they liked the food in Africa, what they did for fun, whether they obeyed their parents—and the people seemed delighted by their answers. When the meal arrived, Lydia was starving, and dove into her food.

"Good job, Lydia," her dad whispered to her.

"What?"

"For eating that so well," he said. "You honor them."

Lydia shrugged. "It's good!"

"Really? That slimy stuff is actually pig skin."

Lydia stopped, set down her plate, and felt green.

Frank looked worried. "I shouldn't have told you. Keep eating."

She couldn't have eaten more if she'd wanted to. As it was, she had trouble not throwing up. Puking probably wouldn't honor them.

"Fine," her dad whispered, looking at her face. "You've eaten enough. Just thank them graciously for their food—and don't vomit!"

"Dad!" she said. "Don't say that."

It took a half hour for Lydia to feel normal again. Just in time.

"Please tell us the purpose of your visit," the old lady said.

"We have come to find a young girl," Frank began.

"What girl?" the woman asked sharply.

"A girl who was taken from her mother in Liberia when she was just five years old," Frank answered cautiously.

"What do you want with this girl?" the old lady asked.

"To bring her news," Frank answered simply.

"What news?"

"Her mother, Arway Benuta, had been holding her little girl in prayer all these years, and had been hoping to find her and bring her back—"

"What if she doesn't want to go back?" the old woman asked.

Frank smiled sadly. "The news we come to pass on is that the mother has died. We simply wanted to pass on Arway's love."

It was true. Before, Lydia had wanted to connect this mother and daughter more than anything. But now, all she could do was give a few memories to Promise. She hoped it would be enough.

The expression on the old lady's face was hard to read. She seemed both sad and relieved. "What girl do you speak of?"

"The name her mother gave her is Promise," Frank said. "She has a birthmark between her eyes. We recently received a tip that she might be in this village." Dad pulled out the piece of paper Big Henry had given him at the clinic five days ago. "Have we arrived in the right place?"

The old lady didn't even glance at the paper, but she nodded. She had not interpreted this last discussion for her people, but she now turned to the others and spoke for a few moments. She turned back to Frank. "The girl is called Kalaitu here among her new family," the woman explained. "She is very precious to us. The reason she did not come to join us in this meal is because she is recovering from malaria."

"Recovering?" Frank asked.

"Yes," the woman answered with a tender smile. "She nearly died three weeks ago; but other good Christian missionaries like yourself delivered medicine just in time."

"Praise the Lord," Frank said.

"Yes," the woman replied. "Praise the Lord. And here she is now."

Lydia turned and saw a smiling girl being carried by a strong young man. She looked too big to be carried, but rather sick. The man was about as tall as her dad. His black hair was braided into dreadlocks. His muscles were not quite as big as Big Henry's, but they were still impressive. Lydia stood up—and the old woman did the same. By the time Promise reached them, everyone was standing and Lydia was crying.

"She's beautiful," Lydia said. "She looks just like Arway."

The old woman called the girl to herself, and Promise happily sat by her side. The old woman whispered something to Promise and the girl's eyes got big. She looked at Lydia.

"Tell her," the old woman told Lydia.

Lydia stepped closer to Promise and took her hand. "I knew your mother," Lydia said.

The old lady translated.

"She was beautiful—just like you," Lydia said, looking only at Promise. "She loved children and would do anything for them. She was my friend."

Lydia hardly noticed the translation and was glad to see the girl responding to her. "Your mother loved you very much and prayed for you every day. She knew God was taking care of you."

The girl said something to Lydia in her own language, and the old woman said, "Thank you for telling me. I pray for her every day, too."

Lydia sat down beside her. "I am so sorry to tell you that she died just a few days ago," Lydia said.

The girl's eyes filled with tears.

Lydia waited a moment, afraid to speak because of the tears that were inside of her. "My mother died, too. When I was about your age."

Promise looked surprised. "She did?"

Lydia nodded. She could guess how this little girl must be feeling. "Do you still cry?"

"Sometimes," Lydia said, not caring — hardly remembering — that her dad and Ben were standing right there. "But I'm getting better."

"I'm glad my mother loved God," Promise said.

"She would be glad that you do," Lydia said.

"I'm going to be a doctor when I grow up."

Lydia smiled. "Good. You will help many people."

"I'm going to help people just like Mr. Bonson does. Do you know Mr. Bonson?"

Lydia looked up at her dad, wide-eyed.

"Yes!" Frank said, excitement all over his face. "The missionary from the airport!" He turned to the old lady. "Is that who gave Promise the medicine?"

The old woman nodded. "He got it to us by the hand of God."

Lydia and her dad laughed. "You can say that again."

"Tell us," Lydia said after the story of the medicine had been told and retold and celebrated by all, "how did you get separated from your mother?"

Promise hugged herself and began to speak, but Lydia quickly interrupted. "It's okay. If it's too hard to talk about, you don't have to tell me."

"No, no," the girl said. "I want to tell you. I was very afraid then, but I'm not afraid anymore."

Promise began her tale and the old woman translated. As the words hung in the air, Lydia could almost see the scene happening like a movie in her head.

Promise was only four when her dad died. She remembered looking at his thin face and knowing he wasn't alive anymore. Her mother had been so sad, and even when Promise drew a pretty picture of the three of them together, her mother had cried. Soon, however, her mother became happy again and so Promise was happy again, too.

During the day Promise would play with her friends while her mother sold vegetables at the market, and at night they cuddled together in the same bed. Promise felt very safe . . . until the night the rebels came—the night before Promise's fifth birthday.

Promise woke up to gunshots and terrible screaming. Her mother began to scream, too, when they saw the fighting below. Soldiers were shooting men and pulling the clothes off women and cutting babies and capturing children.

"The rebels!" Arway whispered to her daughter. "We must run."

Fire blocked their escape from the rooftop where they had been sleeping. Arway ran to the edge of the house. Promise begged her mother not to jump, but Arway clutched the girl in her arms and plunged them both down to the hard sand below.

When Promise looked back she saw that the whole house was on fire, and the flames were just starting to reach the roof. She didn't know what happened to her grandfather and grandmother and other relatives who had been sleeping below, but her mother wouldn't let her find out. "We must run," she kept saying.

And they did run. They ran toward the trees outside the clearing of the village, but Promise's mother stumbled. Her leg had been hurt from the jump and she couldn't keep going.

"Take her," Arway pleaded with another village woman who was running. "Please take her." There was no time for questioning, and Promise was whisked away.

A few days later, Promise saw her thirteen-year-old cousin in the next village. Rebels had come to raid this town, too, and her cousin, whom she thought had died in the fire, was now holding a gun and working with the rebels—killing her new friends.

"Joseph," she called to him, crying, "stop!"

He heard her voice and ran to her amid the chaos. "Run, Promise," he said as tears streamed down his face. "I have to shoot or they will do wicked things to me. Please run! I will protect you until you get to the woods."

And Promise ran. All alone. With no mother, no father, and no friend to help her. She looked back to see Joseph staring at her, and then he turned away. She never saw another of her family members again.

Hours later Promise was sleeping in the forest when she woke up to the sound of breaking sticks. A large man in camouflage clothing had placed a tall gun right beside her and had started pulling berries from a nearby bush. He had big muscles and a bald head.

Just as he was about to put them in his mouth, Promise spoke. "Don't eat those," she said—and the man jumped. "Those will make your tummy bad. Eat those." She pointed to some other berries a little way away.

He grabbed his gun and pointed it at her. "You first." She did. "Okay, that's enough." He stared at her suspiciously as he ate the berries hungrily. A twig snapped nearby, and the man jerked his head up. When nothing else happened he demanded, "Where's your family?"

"I don't know," she said. She went over to his leg and hugged it. "Will you help me find them?"

The man started to kick her off, saying, "I can't help you," but suddenly stopped. He sighed deeply. "But I can tell you where to go." He handed her a metal circle and showed her the arrows on it. "Keep walking in a straight line so that the arrow always points to this letter. Always. Keep walking for a long, long time, and you will finally come to another village. You will be able to stay there."

Now, three years later, in the village he'd directed her to, Promise pulled that same compass out of her pocket.

"I keep this to help me remember to always walk in the right direction," she said. "I will never forget."

Saying goodbye to Promise wasn't as hard as Lydia thought it would be. The girl had been through so much, but she was going to be all right. She was going to be more than all right.

Lydia had given Promise memories, but Promise had given Lydia hope.

# 15

# Cross-Eyed

ad news," Frank said Tuesday morning, back at the VanderHooks'. Ben and Lydia were sitting at the kitchen table.

"What?" Lydia said.

"Your diamond isn't real."

"What?"

"The diamond you gave me," Frank continued. "Mrs. Hinkle took it to a jeweler downtown to have it appraised. It's worth about a hundred dollars." He held out his hand and handed it back to her. "I'm sorry."

Lydia accepted the ring back and stared at it. Not real? What did that mean? Did it mean her special moment with God was fake, too? She shook her head. No way. That had been real no matter what.

"Okay," she said, putting the ring in her pocket.

"Okay?" her dad repeated. "That's all?"

"What else is there to say?" But she couldn't hide her disappointment. God was still very real, but it felt like her mother was slipping away.

Lydia needed to get her mind off the ring. She turned her attention back to the treasure hunt. She and Ben went to find Dr. VanderHook's medical license. He was working with patients, so the timing was perfect. They crept into his office. It was Lydia's job to guard the door so Ben could go through his files. Unfortunately, they forgot to decide what to do if someone came.

"Oh, hi, Dr. VanderHook," Lydia said when he came around the corner. To her credit, she spoke quite loudly, hoping to give Ben some warning. But she didn't give much effort to actually guarding. If Dobermans or pit bulls were guard dogs, Lydia was more like a Chihuahua or a poodle. Her yipping didn't help at all. Deep in thought, Dr. VanderHook walked right into his office with hardly a hello to Lydia—and caught Ben in the act.

"What are you doing?" he demanded.

"Ummm . . ." Ben began, standing up quickly. He looked at Lydia.

There was no way Lydia was going to cover for Ben to his own dad. She just shrugged helplessly.

"Ben, why are you going through my files?" Dr. VanderHook asked again.

"It's complicated, Dad," Ben said.

"What are you looking for?" the doctor asked, still seeming more surprised than angry. "It can't be that complicated."

"Ummm . . . your medical license."

Dr. VanderHook pointed to a laminated card the size of a drivers' license stuck in the corner of a framed photograph hanging over his desk. "It's right there. Why do you need it?" Then he held up a hand. "Forget it. Tell me later. I don't have time for this right now. Give me my desk back."

Ben quickly moved over to the door.

"And you *will* tell me later," Ben's dad said with an edge in his voice.

Lydia and Ben scampered out of the room. "That was crazy," Lydia said.

"Some help you were!" Ben said.

"What was I supposed to say?" Lydia asked.

"I don't know. You could have used your drama skills to come up with something," Ben said.

"Lie?" Lydia asked.

"Not lie—just come up with some other excuse," Ben said.

"Lie," Lydia repeated. "No way. I'm not lying to your dad. He's got to have saint status or something in heaven," Lydia said. "Besides, why did we have to sneak around for this anyway? We could have just asked."

"My dad doesn't do fun things like your dad does," Ben said. "He wouldn't understand."

Lydia plunked down on the back steps of the house, soaking up the sunshine. By now she was used to the humidity, and even kind of enjoyed it. "Well, maybe we should just quit then."

"No!" Ben burst out. "Are you kidding? Dad has his way of helping people, and this is my way. Once we get those diamonds—"

"Just kidding," Lydia said. "We need to see the license. And soon. I'm leaving tomorrow."

"Let's go back," Ben said.

"Where?"

"To Dad's office. Let's look at his license."

"He'll kill us!"

"No, he won't," Ben assured, standing up. "More likely maim us. Come on."

Dr. VanderHook had already left his office and gone back into the clinic. "Phew," Lydia said. "Now let's do this quick."

They didn't dare to remove the card from where Dr. VanderHook had it, so they climbed up on the desk and looked at the license from there. It was nothing special. Dr. VanderHook's mug shot was placed in the top left corner and the blanks were filled in with his information.

REPUBLIC OF LIBERIA
LIBERIA MEDICAL BOARD
MINISTRY OF HEALTH AND SOCIAL WELFARE
MONROVIA, LIBERIA

TEMPORARY LICENSE No. _853_
VALID FROM _8/06_ TO _8/07_

THIS IS TO CERTIFY THAT
DR _____ *Peter VanderHook* _____
is duly registered with the Liberia Medical Board,
Ministry of Health & Social Welfare.
He/She is licensed to practice _medicine and surgery_ at
**_Global Relief and Outreach_** Clinic / Hospital
Only and is entitled to rights and privileges granted to
Physicians and Surgeons under the laws of Liberia,
and privileges granted to Physicians and Surgeons.

Peter VanderHook                    Walter Flomo
_____        _____
Holder                     Chairman, Liberia Medical Board

"I don't get it," Lydia said. "How could this be a clue when the treasure hunt was written before your dad even got here?"

"It can't be anything about him specifically," Ben said. "It has to be something that would be on every medical license."

"Right," Lydia said.

They stared at the card some more.

"Let's copy it down so we can get out of here," Lydia suggested.

Ben grabbed a pen and paper.

"Make sure you copy it word for word," Lydia said. "It has to be perfect."

They took the copy back to their room and sat down to work. Ben set the copied medical license aside and pulled the postcard out of his pillow. He started copying the tiny letters out on another piece of paper.

OJ _SG MS_B MOEBHOR, IS VS SMUBWV ON
WRWCRVS_N LSH VCB LONRM PMGB.

"I'm just glad this code has to do with letters and not numbers," Lydia said.

"Yes, but it's all about logic," Ben said. "This weird message I've just copied out from the postcard, it's the code, right?"

"Yeah," Lydia said.

"And the words on the medical license are somehow supposed to show us what these letters mean."

"How?"

Ben shrugged. "That's what we have to figure out."

They spent the next half hour staring at the letters until Lydia felt cross-eyed.

"Maybe we should figure out which words would be on every license," Ben said, "because we were allowed to find any old license, not one that belonged to someone specific."

"Good idea," Lydia said.

"That means basically all the words except the blanks and signatures," Ben said. "I'm not sure about the word 'temporary.' It might not be on permanent licenses."

"Let's leave it out then."

"Okay," Ben said. His eyes lit up. "Hey, we have to figure out what each letter in the code really stands for, right?"

"Yeah . . ."

"Look," Ben said. "You can see that this is a sentence . . ." He pointed to the enlarged clue: OJ _SG MS_B MOEBHOR, IS VS SMUBWV ON WRWCRVS_N LSH VCB LONRM PMGB.

"Yeah," Lydia said, starting to get it, "just with substitute letters."

"Right," Ben said. "Kind of like typing your name and choosing 'symbol' for your font."

"Have you ever done that?" Lydia asked.

Ben's eyes suddenly darted away from hers, and he blushed.

"You did?" Lydia said. "I want to try it! Let me use your computer!"

Ben rolled his eyes, but moved out of her way. While she booted up the laptop (using battery power), Ben stared at the clues in front of him.

"Cool!" Lydia exclaimed, staring happily at the two names on the screen: Λψδια Βαρνεσ

Ben wasn't listening. "I got it!" he yelled.

"No fair!" Lydia said. "I wanted to help. Start over!"

Ben groaned. "Lydia, you're insane."

She grinned. "Thanks. Now what did you figure out?"

"I think," he said, "I *think* we can figure out what the code alphabet is by putting these letters alongside the traditional alphabet." He grabbed a piece of paper and began writing his ABCs in a column down the left-hand side of the page. Then he picked up the copy of the license and put the first letter beside the A, the second letter beside the B, and so forth.

| | | | |
|---|---|---|---|
| A | = R | G | = I |
| B | = E | H | = C |
| C | = P | I | = O |
| D | = U | J | = F |
| E | = B | K | = L |
| F | = L | | |

"Wait!" Lydia interrupted. "You already used an *L*. I think you should go to the next letter that hasn't been used."

Ben leaned in closer to the paper, clearly excited. "I think we're on the right track, Lyd," he said. He erased the *L* and changed it to *A*, then kept writing, checking over the list frequently.

$$K = A \qquad S = W$$
$$L = M \qquad T = V$$
$$M = P \qquad U = G$$
$$N = N \qquad V =$$
$$O = S \qquad W =$$
$$P = T \qquad X =$$
$$Q = Y \qquad Y =$$
$$R = H \qquad Z =$$

"Uh oh!" Ben said. "Maybe we're wrong. There aren't enough letters."

"Rats!" Lydia said. "Let's just try it anyway."

Ben grabbed the code. OJ _SG MS_B MOEBHOR, IS VS SMUBWV ON WRWCRVS_N LSH VCB LONRM PMGB.

He started copying the letters down:

$$O =$$
$$J =$$

"What's with the line?" Lydia asked.

"Who knows," Ben said. "We may be way off track. Let's keep going."

| | | | |
|---|---|---|---|
| _ = | $I$ = | $W$ = | $L$ = |
| $S$ = | $S$ = | $R$ = | $O$ = |
| $G$ = | | $W$ = | $n$ = |
| | $V$ = | $C$ = | $R$ = |
| $m$= | $S$ = | $R$ = | $m$ = |
| $S$ = | | $V$ = | |
| _ = | $S$= | $S$ = | $P$ = |
| $B$ = | $m$ = | _ = | $m$ = |
| | $U$ = | $n$ = | $G$ = |
| $m$ = | $B$ = | | $B$ = |
| $O$ = | $W$ = | $L$ = | |
| $E$ = | $V$ = | $S$ = | |
| $B$ = | | $H$ = | |
| $H$ = | $O$ = | | |
| $O$ = | $n$ = | $V$ = | |
| $R$ = | | $C$ = | |
| | | $B$ = | |

"All right," Lydia said. "Now let's use our code key to fill it in."

"Right," Ben said, pulling up his other sheet of paper. "*O* in the code corresponds to . . . *I* in the alphabet. So . . ." He wrote.

$$O = I$$
$$J = F$$

"It's a word! *If*!" Ben said. "Maybe we're right!"

"Yes, but what's the blank?"

Ben shrugged. "A blank. Let's leave it." He kept filling in the code using the translator key.

```
 _        L
 O        I
 U        B
          E
 L        R
 O        I
 _        A
 E
```

"That says Liberia!" Lydia whispered with excitement. "It's working! You were right."

# 16
# Slimy Snot

Ben said nothing as he continued deciphering, but his fingers were shaking. When he finished, he began reading. "If ou—"

"If *YOU*," Lydia said. "And look—" she pointed to the decoder with no letters after the *Y*.

"If you *lope*?" Ben guessed.

"*Lode*?" Lydia said.

"No, wait," Ben said. "It has to be a letter with a blank. *LOVE!*"

"'If you love Liberia, go to oldest in Sashatown for the final clue,'" Lydia read.

"Sashatown?" Ben repeated.

"That's all?" Lydia asked.

"That sounds hard to me," Ben said. "We don't even know where Sashatown is or how to get there."

"I mean, once we get this, we really find the treasure?" Lydia said.

"It sounds that way."

"Wow. It's weird to think how close we are."

"It's great!" Ben yelled, letting his excitement out by jumping on the bed.

Lydia, though, suddenly felt kind of worried. "Sort of," she said.

"Sort of?" Ben stopped his romp as suddenly as he'd started it.

"Yeah," Lydia said, remembering the conflict over the diamond ring she had given to her dad. "What if we find the treasure, but it actually ruins everything rather than helping everything?"

"What do you mean?"

"It's just that a whole lot of money like that will get people fighting," Lydia explained. "One person will want to use it one way and someone else will want to use it another way."

"That won't happen," Ben said. "Besides, there will be enough for everyone."

"It's like a disease. Maybe worse than AIDS," Lydia said. "I even have it, Ben." She didn't know if she would regret saying this, but she went forward anyway. "A part of me hopes to find it just so that I can have plenty of money to buy stuff for myself!"

Ben cringed. "Yeah, I guess that's crossed my mind, too."

Lydia continued. "If the person who set up these clues knew that we were just some kids who might not use it right, I wonder—"

"But, Lydia," Ben interrupted, "he does know that we're the right people to find the treasure!"

"What do you mean? How could he possibly—"

"Because the only way we could solve the riddle is if certain things were in place."

"What do you mean?" Lydia asked.

"Read this," he said, pointing to the clue they had just found. "He wants to make sure that we love Liberia. If we don't, then we can't solve the riddle."

"Hmm," Lydia said, scanning the clue. "I guess that was true for the clue we got from Big Henry, too. We could only get it if we were Christians."

"I don't know what this one we got from the medical license proves," Ben said.

"Or the Temple of Justice," Lydia added.

"Well, we couldn't have solved the first clue if the corrupt people were still in power—in other words, if the country was still at war," Ben explained. "We wouldn't have been allowed in that place."

"I still don't get it, though," Lydia said. "I don't get what he is trying to make sure of."

"Oh, well," Ben said. "Let's go finish this treasure hunt."

They went looking for Lydia's dad, but Mrs. VanderHook told them he was not to be disturbed as he was finishing up his paperwork. So they decided she would have to do.

"Sure, I'll take you there," Mrs. VanderHook said after they had explained everything. "This is rather exciting!"

"Where's Sashatown, though?" Ben asked.

"I know right where that is—just an hour or so from here. It's near where they built that new school we went to last year, remember?"

"Oh yeah!" Ben said. "When can we go?"

"It works for me to go right now," Mrs. VanderHook said. "Does that work for you?"

"Yes!" both kids responded.

"Well, then, let me see if Gretchen wants to come," Mrs. VanderHook said.

Mrs. Hinkle! No way! "Umm," Lydia quickly interjected, "can we go with just the three of us?"

"You afraid she'll give you more math homework?" Mrs. VanderHook joked. "Don't worry. It'll be fine." She walked away to find Hink.

"This is terrible!" Ben said.

"What are we going to do?" Lydia asked.

"There is nothing we can do," Ben said. "We just have to be sure Hink doesn't catch wind of the fact that we're trying to get the last clue.

Hink didn't have to "catch wind." Mrs. VanderHook was telling her everything! "And so now they're seeking the last clue, which they expect will lead them directly to the treasure," Mrs. VanderHook said as the two women walked toward the kids. "We didn't realize what this was all about in the beginning, but now that we're at the end, it's rather exciting, don't you think?"

Hink looked right at Lydia and smiled wickedly. "Yes, it certainly is."

Lydia groaned.

Mrs. VanderHook knew exactly where to go without even using a map, and even Hink seemed to know her way around. The old lady must have been out searching for clues quite a bit while Ben and Lydia were out of her clutches. And now they were handing her this last one on a silver platter. Hink was smiling slightly, and she seemed to look hungrily at the surroundings as they passed through the countryside—as if she could almost taste her own success. Well, not if Lydia could help it.

For now, though, all Lydia could do was look out the window and wait. And, if she could overlook the military checkpoints that popped up every few miles, it really was gorgeous—banana trees, palm trees, and wide-open space. Refreshing after so much time in the crowded city.

When they arrived in the village of Sashatown, a crowd of kids surrounded them—much like they had in Promise's village. They weren't as poor here, though, Lydia could see. The houses were little, but well kept. Brightly colored clothes hung on the lines. An older man named Tamba came to welcome them, greeting them in the typical Liberian fashion: a loose handshake ending in a snap between both people's middle fingers.

Tamba proudly showed them around his small village. "You must greet the children first," he said as he led them into the open-air schoolhouse.

The children stood up and said in unison, "Welcome, visitors."

Mrs. VanderHook bowed a little and said, "Thank you, students. We are so glad to be here in your beautiful village."

Lydia felt stupid standing in front of all the kids who seemed to expect her to do something.

"Let's give our visitors the gift of song," one of the teachers said, breaking the awkward silence. He nodded to a girl in the front row, who began a beautiful chorus supported by the rest of the students. Lydia could hardly believe how well they performed on the spur of the moment. If a recording of this had been on YouTube, it would have won some award by now.

They stayed in the classroom a bit longer, and each of the guests ended up speaking some words to the class. "It's expected," Mrs. VanderHook whispered to the kids when they tried to refuse. "Say something."

Ben told the students to study hard, that education would help them go far in life. Lydia complimented them on their singing and then got inspired to tell them to trust God to provide for all their needs. Mrs. Hinkle went on for ages about what a wonderful experience it was for her to be in their great country. She then bowed very deeply. Lydia was relieved when they could finally leave.

"Tell me," Tamba said after they strolled around the village for a little while, admiring the two pigs and six ducklings, "what brings you here to our humble village?"

He looked at Mrs. Hinkle, the oldest in the group, but she turned to gesture to the youngest. "This young man has something to ask you."

Lydia had been ready to interrupt Hink just a second ago, and now she could only stare with her jaw open. Ben was at a loss for words, too.

"Go on, Ben," Mrs. VanderHook prodded.

"We came to tell you that we love Liberia," Ben said.

The man smiled and waited.

"Umm, we *really* love Liberia," Lydia said.

"Good. Good," the man said. "So do I." He still waited, apparently not catching on.

"Sir," Ben said, "are you the oldest person in this town?"

"Yes," the man said. "Only last year my brother Moses Sasha died, and he was the one person older than me—" His eyes suddenly lit up. "Oh!" he said. "You love Liberia!"

Ben and Lydia nodded their heads vigorously and said, "Yes, yes!"

"Come then, and have a meal with me. Then you shall get what you are looking for."

He brought them into a home made from mud walls and a tin roof and seated them at a wooden table in student desk seats. They made small talk for a little while until the man's wife brought a large pan of pink rice and a bowl of green mush.

"This is potato-leaf soup with duiker meat," the man said. "We are honored to share it with you."

It looked about the same as the food Lydia had eaten in the other village, but she tried not to think of that. It really had been good before she had known what it was. And this was good, too. She even accepted seconds. By now the little kids who were not in school had gathered around and laughed as the Americans ate. Lydia found herself feeling more and more comfortable, and would sometimes walk her fingers toward the kids only to send them screaming happily into the corner. The man and his wife only smiled.

"Now, for the best part of all," the man said when everyone had eaten their fill.

Lydia's stomach did a flip. She could hardly wait. Here it was!

The man put a new pot on the table and took off the lid. He held it out before them, with a huge smile spread on his face. "Please, eat," the man said. "The pride of Liberia."

Lydia looked in, and her stomach lurched again—for a totally different reason. The little kids at the table starting reaching in to grab at the slimy goop in front of them, squealing with delight, but the man held them back. "No, no, no," he said. "This is for our guests."

This was not the clue. This was supposed to be dessert. But no matter how she tried, Lydia could not convince herself this oatmeal-colored slippery mass was a piece of chocolate cake. Ben and Lydia stared at each other. They had to eat this? Was this *Fear Factor* meets *Candid Camera*? *I can't eat that,* Lydia tried to say to Ben with her eyes.

"Thank you so much, Tamba," Hink said, smiling sweetly. "I would be honored."

She reached in and pulled out what looked like a hunk of snot and lifted it to her mouth. Everyone watched her chew it for a moment, and then they watched the lump go down her throat. Hink closed her eyes. "Mmm," she said. "Magnificent."

Was she kidding?

"You?" the man asked each of the other guests, but they all said no.

"I wish I could," Mrs. VanderHook said, "but I am completely full."

"No, thank you," was all Lydia and Ben could manage to utter.

The man turned the pot back to Hink, who looked positively happy to dive in for seconds. "I can't believe I discovered this on my last day here," she said. "I wish I could stay forever to enjoy this delicious food every day." She sucked down another bite, and then the waiting children were freed to finish it off—which they did in seconds. "What do you call it?"

"It is called foofoo," Tamba said. "But I have something better than that to give you," he said to Hink. "Please wait here."

*The clue!* Hink ate the goop and earned the next clue! *Nooo!*

"Wait!" Lydia called before he disappeared out of the room. "I'll have some foofoo after all!"

The man smiled and shook his head. "I'm afraid it's all gone, tutu," he said before stepping out of the room.

Lydia looked at Ben—and groaned. How could she have been so stupid?

Moments later the man returned and held a piece of paper in his hands. "This note has passed from eldest to eldest for ten years now. I nearly forgot about it, to tell you the truth." He handed the note to Hink and bowed deeply. "Your passion for Liberia is evident, ma'am," he said. "I hope this is of great use to you."

Hink took the note and bowed back. "I'm much obliged," she said.

She turned to Ben and Lydia and grinned.

# 17
# Mother Lode

They were beaten. Hink had won. And there was nothing either Ben or Lydia could do. Lydia's first reaction was to jump up and grab the note, but she wisely resisted. After all, Mrs. Hinkle had won it fair and square—and making a scene would not help anyone. Besides, Hink was probably stronger than she looked.

Lydia's second reaction was to cry. She nearly did that, but then the strangest thing happened.

"Which one of you wants this?" Hink asked as soon as they had said their goodbyes and climbed into the Pathfinder.

Lydia didn't understand the question at first, but when Hink held out the note, Lydia nearly screamed. She wanted that clue so much her fingers were burning, but she pointed to Ben. "He does," she said, voice trembling. He had done most of the work for this, after all. And it seemed to matter more to him.

Ben looked like he was going to faint again.

"Take it, Ben," she said, shoving him.

Ben took it.

"Open it!" Lydia said.

Ben opened it.

*Four pieces apart make a puzzle.*
*Four pieces together solve one.*

"What does that mean?" Mrs. VanderHook asked.

"This is better than algebra," Hink said.

Lydia looked at her teacher as if for the first time. "You really do love math, don't you?"

"You bet I do!" the old lady said.

"And you really do love Monrovia." It wasn't an act.

"You thought I was a fake?" Hink asked.

Lydia blushed. Why did she always blush at the wrong time?

"That's okay," Hink said. "I forgive you."

"We even thought you were after the treasure," Lydia said.

Mrs. VanderHook laughed. "Why did you think that?"

Lydia looked at her teacher. "You were at the Y when we were there and you just, well, seemed to be . . ." Lydia ran out of words again.

"*I* sent her to the Y!" Mrs. VanderHook said. "To greet the new director on our behalf."

So she hadn't been lying.

"I got it!" Ben said, abruptly changing the subject. "We need all four clues. They must fit together like a puzzle."

"What do you mean?"

"Read the clue," he said, handing it to her. "*Four pieces apart make a puzzle. Four pieces together solve one*."

"Oh, no," Lydia said. "The first clue got stolen!"

"Stolen?" Mrs. VanderHook asked.

"Yeah," Ben said. "The night Lydia and them arrived, some-one broke into our house and took it from my room."

Mrs. VanderHook chuckled. "No one broke into the house," she said. "That was me."

"What?"

"I woke up in the middle of the night thinking of all the things I had to do the next day. I always write down a list when that happens so that I can fall asleep."

"So you took my clue?" Ben asked.

"Well, first I went downstairs to find a notepad, but I think I woke Lydia up."

Lydia smiled. So that's who the intruder had been.

Mrs. VanderHook went on. "I didn't like to bother her, and since you sleep like a hibernating bear, Ben, I decided to get something from your room. You have nothing but junk in your room, young man," she said, shaking her head. "I don't know how you can think straight. Did you find that he was completely unorganized, Gretchen—"

"Mom! Did you take the clue?"

Mrs. VanderHook shrugged. "I straightened things up a bit, and then I finally found some paper. I don't know if your 'clue' was part of that."

"Where is that paper now?"

"Oh, I don't know," Mrs. VanderHook said. "Maybe it's still in my room."

Everything depended on that maybe.

It was a good thing it didn't depend on speed because Mrs. VanderHook drove like she were being towed by a snail. It took three million years to get back to the VanderHooks' house.

When they finally made it, Ben and Lydia tore up the stairs.

"Wait!" Ben's mom called from below them. "Don't just go barging into my bedroom. I'll look. Hold on a second."

Ben and Lydia sat on the top step side by side while Mrs. VanderHook took her sweet time making whatever preparations she needed to begin the long journey up the staircase. When she finally arrived, Ben and Lydia were nearly twitching with anticipation.

"I think I know where it might be," Mrs. VanderHook said. "I'll be right back."

More waiting.

It was well worth it, though. A moment later Ben's mom handed him a small stack of papers with the first clue nestled in the middle of the pile.

Ben and Lydia grabbed each other and hugged while dancing in a circle. When Ben nearly fell down the stairs, they quit the celebration and ran to Ben's room, where they pulled out the other clues.

"Good thing we never got around to destroying the second clue," Ben said as he pulled out of his desk drawer the note they'd found in the plastic bag at the Temple of Justice. "Sometimes it's good to put things off. I'll have to tell my mom that when she asks me to sweep the floor."

They spread the clues on the floor of Ben's room: the scrambled letters that had directed them to the Temple of Justice, the postcard with the LMB code, the Big Henry message, the medical license (which Ben had run downstairs to beg from his dad), and the last note from Tamba Sasha.

"It doesn't look like a puzzle," Lydia said.

"And there are five pieces, not four," Ben said. "Which one don't we use?"

"Which one doesn't fit in?"

"That's what I just said!" Ben sounded a bit frustrated. Being so close to the solution must have been getting to him.

"Well, not exactly," Lydia said. "I was thinking of one of those stupid games we used to play as kids. You know, when you look at four images, all of them almost exactly the same, and try to figure out which one is different."

"I guess that would be the medical license then," Ben said.

"It's the only laminated one."

"It's also the only one the guy who planned the treasure hunt didn't make himself," Lydia added.

Ben set the medical license aside. "So how do these four fit together?" he asked.

"They're all the exact same shape," Lydia said.

"Right," Ben said. "This is no jigsaw puzzle."

"So what will connect them?" Lydia asked. "Is there anything on the back?"

Ben flipped them over. "I don't see anything." He picked up the magnifying glass and leaned in close over the first clue. "Hey!" he shouted. "There is something here!"

"I'm right beside you," Lydia said. "You don't need to yell."

Ben's nose was almost touching the desk. "There are some letters here that are in a pie shape in the bottom right-hand corner. The first row is HEKITC. The second row is HECHR. The next row is EKOU. Then MB. Then I." He reached for the second clue and put it to the right of the first one.

"What do you see?" Lydia demanded.

"It connects!" he shouted. "The first row here is HENUNDE, and carried over from the second line of the first clue, it makes the word KITCHEN." Ben looked some more and then said, "The word under that is CHRISTIAN, but none of the other letters seem to connect."

"Get the other clues!" Lydia said.

Ben looked at the postcard with the magnifying glass and spotted the letters in the top right-hand corner. He put the piece into place, and then placed the final clue they just received in the bottom right-hand corner.

"You look," he said. "I'm shaking too much."

Lydia didn't need to be told twice.

THE SINK PR24 IN THE CHRISTIAN CLINIC POINT ON SEKON TOURE AVE IN MAMBA IN THE KITCHEN UNDER

"Kitchen unde . . ." she began slowly. But then she saw it: "under the sink! PR24, which must be Proverbs 2:4 again! Let me read the rest. It must start right at the corner of the page." She began: "In Mamb—wait, we need to tape these together."

"We don't have any. We're in Monrovia, remember? It's not like we can just go run to OfficeMax."

"Oh, yeah," Lydia said. "Okay, I'll just turn my head." She read slowly: "IN MAMBA POINT ON SEKOU TOURE AVE IN THE CHRISTIAN CLINIC IN THE KITCHEN UNDER THE SINK PROVERBS 2:4."

"Here?" Ben said, clearly shocked. "The treasure is here?"

"Amazing," Lydia said. She shrugged.

"Under the sink, though?" Ben asked. "How could a diamond mine fit under our sink?"

"Let's go find out," Lydia said.

Mrs. VanderHook was busy making supper when Ben and Lydia started hauling cleaning supplies out from under the sink. "Now what?" she asked.

"Lydia!" Ben hollered. "It's right here! A trap door!"

"That's not a trap door, Ben," Mrs. VanderHook said. "I spotted that a long time ago. "There's just a shallow little compartment under there. It's empty."

Ben's narrow eyes got narrower. "Empty?" he said.

"Let's look anyway," Lydia said. She had lost hope herself, but Ben looked so upset that she had to do something.

"Nah. Why bother?" he said.

"Come on, Ben," Lydia said. "What could it hurt?"

But Mrs. VanderHook was right: The compartment was empty. And now she was complaining about their getting in her way. "Put it away now, kids," she said. "Everyone will be coming in here in just a moment—"

"Ben!" Lydia said, not meaning to cut off a grownup but too excited to stop herself. "Ben! Look!" She had been poking her fingers around the compartment, hoping to find a clue or something, when one of the boards tilted. "There's more!"

Sure enough, she could feel a latch underneath the tilted board. When she managed to unclip the latch several minutes later, the compartment came loose, and together they pulled it up.

Underneath was another trap door.

The latch was jammed, impossible to open.

"Let me help," Frank said. Lydia hadn't noticed his arrival, but she could see that he was just as excited as they were.

He helped by smashing the lock with a hammer and then pulling the heavy door up and out of the cupboard under the sink.

"Here's a flashlight," Dr. VanderHook said. Lydia hadn't noticed *him* arrive, either. Everyone was being awfully quiet.

Ben took the flashlight and peered down. "I can't see anything. We have to go down."

"Is there a ladder?" Hink asked.

"Yes."

"Do you want to go first, Ben?" the doctor asked.

Ben nodded silently. "If that's all right."

His dad nodded. "Just test each rung before you put your full weight on it."

Ben nodded again and swung one leg over the edge.

"There might be rats or spiders or something down there," Mrs. VanderHook said.

Everyone ignored her. Ben kept going.

Lydia went next.

They moved out of the way of the ladder to avoid the dust that was falling on them from above as her dad came down.

Ben shone his flashlight to reveal a small room, about half the size of Ben's bedroom, that appeared to be hand dug. The walls were dirt, though the floor was covered in a wooden platform. Along the walls were sturdy shelves filled with boxes.

"Man alive!" Frank said quietly. "I wonder what it is."

"Not diamonds," Ben said.

"Let's get one of them upstairs," Frank said. He took one box off the shelf and handed it up the ladder to Dr. VanderHook.

The three people below stood solemnly, still looking around.

"Oh, Lord!" Dr. VanderHook exclaimed from above a moment later. "Oh, Lord!"

Ben was the first one up the ladder. "What, Dad? What is it?"

Lydia and her dad were right behind him.

"It's an antiretroviral—a medication that stops the replication of retroviruses," the doctor said, clearly shocked.

"To treat AIDS?" Hink asked.

"Yes," the doctor said, getting excited now. "There is more in this one box than I had available to me all last year. Incredible!"

"Has it expired?" Mrs. VanderHook asked, unbelieving.

"No!" the doctor replied. "It doesn't expire for another three years, and it's been stored beautifully. Whoever hid this knew what he was doing." The doctor put a hand through his hair and smiled. "Good job, Ben." Tears sprang to the doctor's eyes.

Ben smiled back. "Lydia helped a lot."

"And so did Mrs. Hinkle," Lydia said.

She was surprised to see Hink smile shyly.

"Well, let's get down there and see what else this team has conjured up," Dr. VanderHook said with a huge grin. "Give me that flashlight." A few minutes later he called up, "If this is all labeled accurately, which seems likely, we've hit the mother lode. We've more antiretroviral than I dreamed possible. This is expensive stuff."

"Let me down there, Pete," Frank called. "I'll hand the stuff up to you."

They traded places, and Frank handed box after box up to Mrs. VanderHook and Hink who brought them to the table where Dr. VanderHook inspected them. Once approved—and every single box proved to be well preserved—the doctor handed them off to Ben and Lydia, who took them to the storage room in the clinic.

When dinner was finally served several hours later, the dirty, sweaty, happy gang of men, women, and teens celebrated with great delight.

"I can't believe we have to leave tomorrow," Hink said sadly. "I don't ever want to leave."

"I wish you could stay, Gretchen," Mrs. VanderHook said. She turned suddenly to Frank. "Won't you give her up, Frank?" the doctor's wife begged. "She would be such a help to us."

Frank looked as surprised as a Californian in a snowstorm. Hink stay? "Are you serious?" he asked.

"I could be," Mrs. VanderHook responded. She looked at her husband. "Now that we have all this medicine, don't you think we'll be able to increase our efforts here? We'll need more help. And we have plenty of room for Gretchen to stay in the spare bedroom."

Dr. VanderHook turned to look at Hink. "Is my wife meddling into your life, or is this something you want too?"

"I'd love to stay," Hink said quietly. "Liberia has had my heart for many years. I spent two weeks here as a little girl with my parents on a missions trip, and I've always wanted to come back. It's as wonderful as I remembered it."

"Hey!" Frank said. "What if I won't give her up?"

"She's not yours to begin with," Mrs. VanderHook said, putting her arm around her friend's shoulders. Hink wrinkled her nose and looked like she might stick out her tongue at Frank.

Frank broke out into a laugh. "I love how God works things out," he said. "I was getting sick of you anyway, Gretchen," he said, as he gently punched her shoulder.

Hink did stick out her tongue this time, and everyone laughed.

"Does this mean I don't have to do school anymore?" Lydia asked.

"Of course it doesn't mean that," Frank said. "We're almost to Christmas break, which we'll take while we're in Israel, but when we get back we'll find someone meaner and tougher than Hink to keep you in line."

Everyone laughed again.

"I'll email Cynthia to see about getting you a salary, Gretchen," Dr. VanderHook said.

"I don't mind volunteering," Hink said. "In exchange for room and board, that is."

"That's very gracious," Dr. VanderHook said, "but out of the question. Anyway, we'll get the details worked out soon. For now, welcome aboard."

Even Ben offered a cheer when his dad lifted his cup—only to roll his eyes at Lydia a moment later and to whisper, "Can you believe I'm stuck with the Hink?"

As she stood at the airport saying goodbye to everyone, Lydia wished she had thought to get a present or something for Ben. He had turned out to be one awesome friend. She would miss him.

"Can't we exchange Mrs. Hinkle for Ben?" she asked after hugging her new buddy goodbye for the third time. She was serious, but everyone else laughed. It would have been so fun to have more adventures with Ben in other countries.

"Oh, well," Ben said. "Take lots of pictures. Israel sounds amazing. Especially at Christmastime."

It did sound amazing, and even though she was sad to leave Monrovia, she had to admit she was looking forward to this next trip. They were laying over in Amsterdam for one night, and she and her dad would most definitely explore that territory. Better yet, she'd be able to take a hot shower!

The flight turned out to be pleasantly boring. Lydia slept most of the time. All of their luggage arrived and they made it to the hotel without mishap.

"Come downstairs with me, Peachoo," her dad said after they were both cleaned up—which took awhile because Lydia stood forever in the hot running water. "Let's have a nice dinner in the restaurant."

Her dad stopped at the front desk of the luxurious hotel before heading to the restaurant and asked for a package. Lydia couldn't stop looking around. Besides the bright lights and cool air, the floors were shiny and the walls were covered with wallpaper or drapes or huge paintings. Fancy couches and chairs were scattered around the lobby.

"Yes, sir," the clerk said. "We've kept it safe and sound for you." He winked.

Frank smiled and took Lydia's hand. "Come here, Peachoo." He sat her down in a quiet corner of the lobby, reached into the yellow manila envelope, and pulled out a small gift-wrapped box. "Open it."

Lydia hugged her dad. "You're awesome, Dad!" she said. "I can't believe you had a gift sent here for me."

"Just open it, baby," he said.

Lydia tore the paper off and dropped it beside her on the floor. She opened a little black case—to discover a heart-shaped diamond pendant hanging daintily on a silver chain. She gasped.

"It's the diamond your mother bought for you all those years ago," her dad said quietly.

Lydia couldn't say anything. She felt a rock-like lump in her throat. "Dad," she finally whispered, touching the diamond with one finger.

"I never finished the story," he said. "We couldn't buy that first diamond your mother saw, but she was determined to get you an heirloom. We must have walked ten miles that day searching out the perfect diamond for you. I thought she was crazy, but I see now how important that was."

Lydia took the necklace out of the velvet box and opened the clip. Her dad took it from her hands and slipped it around her neck.

"It's crazy how much like your mother you are, Peachoo," he said. "Even without this necklace, her fingerprints are all over you."

"But with this necklace, I can feel them," Lydia said.

As she hugged her dad, she smiled. God certainly had things under control. She would never doubt again.

# Many Thanks to—

Jo Anne Lyon, the inspiration behind this series,
for believing kids can make a difference.

Mary McNeil, (still) my best friend and excellent editor,
for believing *I* can make a difference.

Jeff Gerke,
for teaching me so much about fiction.

The entire team at Wesleyan Publishing House, especially
Don Cady, Lawrence W. Wilson,
Darlene Teague, Mark Moore, Jennette ElNaggar,
Dana Porter, Lyn Rayn, and Jim Pardew.

Larry and Cindy Marshall, development workers in Liberia,
for opening your home and life to me,
and for your faithful ministry around the world.

Lauren Selmon, Lee Gallinger, and Esther Worthington,
for helping to make this book authentic.

Simon Gemmen, Rachael Gemmen, and Jordan Dykstra,
for your expertise on how kids think.